WOMEN UNDER FIRE

GRAYCE WALTERS ROMANTIC SUSPENSE SERIES - BOOK 2

JACKI DELECKI

To my heroes—my husband and my devoted Golden Lab, Talley.

PROLOGUE

Angie stood motionless in the shadow of a misshapen cypress tree. The setting summer sun of Seattle didn't relieve the cold frisson of danger or the press of her revolver's cold metal against her skin. Although it had been months since her last reconnaissance mission, her body recognized the drill and tightened into high alert.

Splatters of fading sunlight danced across the sagging house. Official yellow tape was wrapped around the turn of the century beauty like a Christmas bow on a crushed, forgotten present. A "condemned" sign was nailed to the warped door. The crumbling front steps looked like their weight bearing days were a distant memory.

Not sure how to proceed, she waited and watched the abandoned house in the residential Ravenna neighborhood until it got dark. Should she take the squatters unaware? Surprise Maddy before she could run?

She moved from her hiding place to investigate the back of the house. The yard was littered with broken glass, smashed Styrofoam carryout containers, and plastic bags mired in mud from the wet Northwest summer. She stepped over the yellow tape that was haphazardly hung around the back steps, turned the handle, and then pulled open the back door. It was unlocked. The rusting hinges screeched.

"Maddy, it's Angie from your VA group." She reverted to her forceful military command voice. "I'm coming in."

When the door was thrown wide open, small dark bodies— rats— scurried away. Dread raced down her spine into the tips of her toes. God, she hated rats. This rat hole was worse than anything she had seen during her tours of duty in Afghanistan.

She stepped gingerly over the bags of garbage strewn on the uneven linoleum floor. The smell of the years of neglect and black mold hit her sensitive nose. She tried not to breathe. All of her senses heightened in the darkness, an internal radar honed from door-to-door urban combat. She took another two steps, listening for sounds other than the resident rodents.

"It's Angie from your VA group." She wasn't too worried about handling a high Maddy, but handling her companions might get tricky. After eight years as a Marine, she was used to tricky. And after everything Maddy had gone through in Afghanistan, Angie wasn't about to let her friend descend into another hell.

She reached in the pocket of her jeans for her tiny penlight as she walked into the dark dining room. The light of her flashlight reflected back at her from a cracked mirror hanging over the fireplace, then a sudden, shiny motion. Before she could react, a bright burst of pain exploded in her head. She fought against overpowering blackness.

———

Brandon knew his lair had been invaded. The back door was ajar. The yellow "condemned" tape had been disrupted. Trespassers!

He heard her before he saw her. She was shouting that she was "Angie from the VA."

Another fucking bitch intruding. Women were always invading his space. Outrage surged through him.

"Keep it together...keep it together..." He repeated the words to himself. His therapist had taught him to use words to pace himself before he acted.

Taking the heavy flashlight from its hiding place behind the refrigerator, he stepped softly into the dining room. He edged around the bags to avoid alerting the intruder to his presence.

A tall woman in a camouflage jacket was bending over, inspecting something on the floor.

Why was a single soldier from the VA hospital searching his house? If the authorities had been alerted about the amount of RDX he had stored here, the entire King County Swat team would've been surrounding the house, with help from those ATF Keystone commandos. If you could call that help.

He had no choice. He needed time to clear out.

He cautiously took two steps to stand over her. He slowly raised the flashlight, and she gasped, seeing his reflection in the old mirror that Brandon knew hung over the fireplace. Using his advantage, he swung in a wide arc and bashed the back of her head with all his strength.

CHAPTER ONE

Ambushed by Aunt Aideen, Grayce Walters was trapped. The bonds of social pressure gripped tighter around her wrists and ankles, holding her captive in the kitchen chair. She couldn't escape tonight's séance.

Dressed in a flowing cobalt-blue caftan, Aunt Aideen ceremoniously placed a scarred, black box on the table and then carefully opened a chest lined in red velvet and raised a glimmering crystal ball into the air. "This *Keek-Stane* has been passed down through generations of Scottish witches."

The enormous kitchen suddenly went airless. Grayce gulped for a breath. Mitzi, who had been sleeping under the table, protectively covered Grayce's feet with her paws.

Grayce knew nothing about tarot cards or witches. Why hadn't Davis warned her that his aunt considered herself a witch? Grayce had recognized Aunt Aideen as a gifted intuitive, but not a witch, whatever that meant.

Aunt Aideen placed the ball in the center of the table spread with tarot cards. "The *Keek-Stane* guides me in the reading of the cards."

A call to a suspicious fire had interrupted the cozy dinner with her boyfriend, his aunt and dog. If Davis had stayed, she'd be eating dessert instead of having a metaphysical experience.

Aunt Aideen's enormous moonstone ring flickered in the candle-light as her hand hovered over the cards. "We must look to the future."

Grayce couldn't see the card. She felt light-headed from the burning sweet flag incense or from the ominous energy swirling from the crystal ball.

As she turned over the first tarot card, the large woman's usual booming voice grew quiet with a mysterious Gaelic lilt. "The Knight of Swords."

Prickly sensations lifted the fine hair on Grayce's neck. Mitzi came from under the table and sat next to Grayce's chair.

Aunt Aideen opened her massive hand to allow Grayce to see the card—a medieval knight in armor on a powerful white horse rode toward a battle in the distance. The horse's harness was decorated with butterflies and birds. The sky behind him was filled with storm clouds and the trees, tossed wildly by the wind. The knight resembled St. Michael the Archangel.

"The Knight of Swords is hard to resist," Aunt Aideen intoned.

Davis obviously fit the Knight of Swords. His commanding presence, physical strength, and his commitment to fight crimes made him the perfect archetypal hero.

Heat moved across Grayce's cheeks in embarrassment. "Davis was hard to resist." Grayce knew first hand. As a witness to arson, she had been interviewed by the sexy fire investigator and had fallen in love with the irresistible man.

"My nephew, Ewan Davis, is in no way a Knight of Swords. Davis is an Emperor, a man of the logical world, like his Scottish forebears. The Knight of Swords is a messenger, a call for adventure. He does not see, nor does he care about risks or dangers and instead moves forward with his strong determination and strength to succeed, no matter what.

Grayce wasn't going to discuss Davis' ability as an adventurous lover with the aunt who had raised him after his mother's death.

"The knight will call to you from your dreams." Aunt Aideen's solemn voice and the shimmering moonstone known for clairvoyance were doing strange things to Grayce's perceptions. The images in the room faded in and out. The heightened energy from the ball moved in undulating waves.

"His call will challenge you to leave your present way of being." Aunt Aideen's eyes were in the shadows, but Grayce felt her focused stare. "The Knight of Swords can also be seen as a warning."

With the soft burr of Aunt Aideen's Scottish inflection, the wavering candlelight and the nutty scent of sweet flag, Grayce was floating into deep relaxation.

Aunt Aideen's voice lost its soothing rhythm. "And it doesn't take a seer to predict that Davis will have trouble with the knight's appearance in your life. Davis needs to be your protector."

Grayce came immediately out of her meditative state. Davis tried very hard to control his fear of unforeseen disasters by guarding all those he loved.

"Does the knight have to be human? Maybe I'll have a new patient?" Grayce asked.

Aunt Aideen kept her eyes closed. Her muted voice was firm. "I see a tall, dark man in a uniform. He holds a gun."

Shivers of fear danced on Grayce's skin.

Aunt Aideen's lowered voice vibrated with intensity. "I see difficulty and danger ahead for you and Davis."

Alarm rushed through Grayce, making her legs rubbery and weak behind her knees although she was seated. Mitzi pushed her cold wet nose against Grayce's hand. Aunt Aideen wasn't the kind of woman to predict gloom and doom.

Aunt Aideen's head was bent. Her hands floated above the table then stilled over a card. "As I suspected, the High Priestess card." The moonstone flashed, sending sparks of light across the raised card.

The High Priestess was seated on a throne, a blond Madonna wrapped in blue moonlight.

With her eyes closed, Aunt Aideen placed her hand with the moonstone ring on the High Priestess card. "You will accept the knight's dangerous adventure and restore the needed balance in a disturbed world." Aunt Aideen's fierce voice pulsed in the room.

Grayce's intuition flared. She had the same foreboding, a prescience of danger just like before she had tangled with the Russian mob. She fought against the rising dread. "I'm leaving the danger to Davis. The arson case was enough violence for a lifetime."

"The cards don't lie." Aunt Aideen's strident tone reverberated in Grayce's head.

Grayce had visions, but she never shared them with anyone. She's never dared to predict the future. Life was expected to be complicated—especially when facing a big decision—or maybe something even more dangerous... But what good could come of knowing ahead of time that suffering and pain were going to overwhelm your life?

Aunt Aideen opened her eyes and looked around the room as if she didn't recognize her own Italian tiled kitchen. She looked at Grayce for a second as if she didn't recognize her either.

Aunt Aideen had been in a deep trance when she made her predictions. The older woman had spent years studying the ancient practices in Tibet and India.

"Would you like me to get you something? A glass of water?" Grayce asked.

"No thank you. I'm exhausted. Your cards are very intense." The older woman stood quickly, but her hand trembled when she placed the crystal ball in the box. "Enough perilous predictions for tonight. Davis is going to be very unhappy with me."

Davis wouldn't be mad at the aunt he loved. He teased her about the tarot card readings because he didn't know his aunt was a gifted seer.

"Let me walk you to the door." Aunt Aideen gestured to the door.

They walked in silence except for the sound of Mitzi's nails clicking on the tiled floor.

Like her nephew, Aunt Aideen was over six feet tall and had to bend to hug Grayce. "The predictions will help you prepare. You are very strong. You and Davis will protect each other in the approaching storm."

CHAPTER TWO

Grayce sipped the warm Diet Coke, straight from the hidden stash in the desk drawer in her animal acupuncture office. After Aunt Aideen's predictions and the subsequent nightmares, she was in need of a fix—the familiar comfort of the miracle elixir.

Hollie, her office assistant, emerged through the open door before Grayce could hide the can. "Drinking Diet Coke? What's wrong?"

Wearing black leggings, black military boots, and a black *World of Warfare* t-shirt with an avenging goddess in flames, Hollie looked like one of the characters out of her favorite video game. "It's the missing woman that's got you upset, isn't it? You shouldn't have agreed to see the cat."

"I haven't seen that t-shirt before. Did you design it?"

"You should never have let that Chow bitch browbeat you."

From a shelter for runaway youths, Hollie was a bit rough around the edges, but her gentle heart made up for her brashness.

Grayce arched her eyebrow in reaction to the word "bitch", before she realized that she was mimicking her office assistant. She wanted to laugh out loud at the reversal of roles. Hollie, a young woman of few words, expressed her displeasure by rolling her eyes or arching one of her pierced eyebrows.

"Okay, okay. Chow"—Hollie's head bobbed back and forth in disdain—"doesn't care about Mrs. Hines' suffering or the missing daughter. That two bit...reporter only cares about her story."

Grayce's unique role as an animal acupuncturist who collaborated with the fire department in an arson investigation had been covered in the local press and TV. Emily Chow, a newscaster, had convinced Mrs. Hines that Grayce could find her daughter, who was suffering from PTSD and had disappeared on the streets of Seattle.

"Regardless of our sentiments toward Emily Chow, I want to help Mrs. Hines."

Hollie rolled her dark expressive eyes.

"How about the rest of the day? Any surprises?"

"Mrs. Leary is bringing her new rescue cat at the end of the afternoon. She insisted that you not give her special treatment by making a house visit. She said it was good for her to get out."

Grayce had treated the elderly woman's dying cat several months before and was glad to hear that after Beowulf's death, Mrs. Leary had decided to allow a new cat into her life. A familiar male voice interrupted her thoughts.

"Do I count as a surprise?" Davis leaned against the doorway.

Dressed in a sleek designer suit and tie with his arms crossed, Davis was as gorgeous as James Bond in a tuxedo. Staring like a teenage groupie, she snapped her mouth closed when she realized it hung open. His fitted black suit, crisp ivory shirt, and knotted tie were at odds with his rawboned, rugged looks. He was every woman's fantasy of the barely tamed, dangerous, bad boy.

"Good morning ladies. Am I interrupting a meeting?"

"We just finished," Grayce said.

Hollie made her way across the room with her street swagger and attitude. She slowed when she got close to Davis and inspected him from his polished loafers to his Armani speckle print tie. "Some fine rags. You applying for a job as an undertaker?"

Davis' deep laugh caused his suit to tighten across his broad chest.

Hollie had given Davis the short shrift when he had first brought Mitzi to the office. Her meth-cooking father had made Hollie wary of men. Grayce was convinced it was Davis' devotion to his ex-girlfriend's poodle that won over her touchy office assistant.

"No, I've got a big meeting with the chief today and then a dinner meeting."

Hollie quietly closed the door.

"You didn't tell Hollie that you're going to be promoted to captain today. She'd be impressed." Grayce teased.

Davis crossed the room in three long, powerful strides. He wrapped his arms around Grayce, peering into her eyes. "Honey, I'm sorry I had to desert you last night."

"You didn't desert me. You had a fire."

"Aunt Aideen read your tarot cards after I left, didn't she?"

Grayce nodded. She didn't plan to go into too much detail about the reading since she hadn't processed the experience yet, and she didn't want Davis to be upset with his aunt. She was a big girl and could handle dire warnings.

"Did she scare you? I know how sensitive you are. If she did anything to upset you..."

Grayce bit on her lower lip to hide her amusement at the idea of Davis taking on his formidable aunt.

"Your aunt did read my cards, but she didn't scare me." Grayce avoided sharing the subsequent nightmares.

"Did she predict you would meet a tall, dark, handsome man?"

Grayce swallowed hard. Did Davis already speak with his aunt?

"And once he saw you, he'd fall at your feet?" Davis tightened his grip on Grayce's shoulders, pulling her against his hard body.

Grayce looked up into his laughing eyes. "I fell at your feet, if you remember." At her interview as an arson witness, she had landed flat on her back on the fire station floor when the heel of her Jimmy Choo had wedged into a crack. "You weren't sure if you even liked me at our first meeting."

"You're so wrong, Grayce. I've always liked you...from the minute I caught a glimpse of you lying on the floor with your short little skirt hiked up on your thighs."

A blush crept up her face with the low rumble of pleasure in Davis' voice and the memory of Davis reenacting his fantasy about her little skirt.

He traced her cheekbones with his thumb, following the burning path down her cheeks. "When your face gets flushed, all I can think about is making the rest of you flush. His breath got ragged. "I've got to stop, or I will embarrass myself." His thumb traced the outline of her lips as his eyes lightened in arousal. "I can't believe I can't see you tonight."

"You're going to have a great time with your friends from your old investment company." Davis had left his career as an investment banker when he father was diagnosed with cancer.

There was a discrete knock on the door.

Grayce pulled back, and smoothed the collar on her blouse. "My first patient must be here."

"They were in the waiting room when I came in. Why is there a big guy, police or ex-military in your waiting room?"

"A policeman? I don't know what he does for a living, but he must be Angie's brother."

"I already don't like him."

"What? You haven't met him. How can you not like him?"

"Because you're going to be nice to him, and he's going to be immediately as smitten with you as I was."

Aunt Aideen understood her nephew's suspicions when she had warned Grayce about Davis' reaction to the Knight of Swords. His ex-girlfriend's betrayal had left an indelible scar of mistrust.

"You're the only one I want smitten." She pulled on his tie.

"And I am." His open mouth brushed along the fine hairs on the side of her face.

"Time to see Mrs. Hines."

"She has the missing daughter, right?"

"Yes."

"Why you let that cold hearted b..." Davis stopped himself. He had better control than Hollie but shared her sentiments about Emily Chow.

"Davis, we've already had this discussion. I've got to go."

"My dinner with my former colleagues will go late. These guys know how to enjoy themselves. But I'll see you tomorrow night."

"I'm really looking forward to the Mariners game."

"Liar." He squeezed her. "But I'm looking forward to having you at the game."

He pressed a sweet, tender, see-you-later kiss on her lips. "Don't be too nice to the Hines guy."

"Good luck with your meeting."

In a few strides, he was gone.

CHAPTER THREE

Angie rolled to her side and then onto her knees. Everything was black and silent, the only sensation a putrefying smell, like burning flesh. Burning flesh? How did she know the smell of burning flesh?

A sharp pain cut between her eyes; bile rose from her gut to her throat. Icy chills pricked her skin. Shit, she fought against the black cloud descending, struggled not to pass out. She stayed on her knees with her neck flexed, waiting out the rolling nausea.

She searched with her hands on the uneven floor, striking the concrete block propped next to her. Where was she? Dazed, she tried to concentrate. She searched for a memory. Nothing came. It hurt to think. Her head throbbed as if she'd been hit with the butt of a rifle.

She pushed to standing and waited for the room to stop swaying and for her head to stop pounding.

She was glad for the darkness since she knew that light would hurt like a son of a bitch. Concrete blocks and bags of garbage surrounded her feet.

Niggling at the back of her mind was a flitter of a memory. She slowly walked toward the light coming through the back door. She swallowed against the gag rising in her throat.

Throwing open the back door, she walked into the sunlight. The pain hit her right between the eyes. Holding onto the doorknob, she waited as the nausea receded.

She stood on the porch, scanning the back yard, searching for a reason why she was in this hellhole.

CHAPTER FOUR

Grayce was in her worst nightmare, and unfortunately she was wide awake.

Aunt Aideen's prediction had sprung to life in her office. Hunter Hines, like the Knight of Swords, with a dark brooding look and military bearing, conveyed impending threat. Sparks of perilous premonition bristled down her spine.

His black, non-descript clothes didn't hide his impressive bulk. Over six feet tall, with the neck of defensive lineman, Hunter Hines was a warrior. Grayce could imagine him as a medieval knight wielding a broadsword.

Grayce listened to his mother with one part of her brain as she tried to sort out the implications of his strange appearance.

"Emily Chow believes that Ossie will tell you where Angie is." Mrs. Hines fervently believed that Grayce could glean the whereabouts of her missing daughter from the cat clutched close to her chest.

"I want to help, but the reporter has exaggerated my abilities," Grayce said.

"When I treat animals with acupuncture, I'm communicating,

but I'm not having a conversation." She never shared or tried to explain her intuitive ability to heal animals. "I'm balancing the animal's energy to help them heal."

Hunter Hines wasn't buying any of this. Giving no hint of sharing his mother's grief, he sat stiff and glared at Grayce across the desk. His contemptuous stare and defiant jaw were aggressive and spoke louder than words.

The older woman stifled a sob into her twisted Kleenex. The raw whimper interrupted Grayce's carefully constructed explanation. "Mrs. Hines, I'll do my best to see if I can learn anything from your daughter's cat."

Grayce walked around her desk and touched Mrs. Hines hand. "Ossie is a beauty."

Mrs. Hines' lips moved upward into a trembling smile. The cat's ears flicked up at the sound of her name.

She spoke directly to Hunter in her most business-like voice, trying to gain control of her need to recoil from his unsettling presence. "How long has Ossie lived with your sister?"

"I don't know. I haven't lived in Seattle for years."

Oblivious to her son's brusque reply, Mrs. Hines answered, "About four years—she just appeared on Angie's deck, obviously starving...just a wee thing." Mrs. Hines spread the gray cat across her lap. "Can you see all her leopard spots?"

The cat's black spots ran in a straight line along her spine. Black stripes etched up her nose and encircled her bright eyes, evoking the look of an exotic Egyptian queen.

"She's some fancy breed called Ocicat. That's how Angie picked her name."

Grayce focused all her attention on the spotted, agouti cat. In comparison to Napoleon, her Maine Coon cat, all cats appeared tiny. Grayce estimated by the long sleek body that Ossie weighed approximately five pounds. Her striking markings and her Abyssinian posture reflected impressive breeding.

"Ossie's usually not this friendly to other people. She only warmed up to me while Angie was deployed in Afghanistan. Angie always said Ossie was her soul-mate and understood everything she said." Her voice quivered. "That's why I thought you could help us."

"I'll do my best. Why don't you move to the treatment chair, and I'll treat Ossie on your lap where she's looking very comfortable."

Hunter rose with his mother and waited while she moved to the overstuffed, chintz chair. His chiseled face registered no warmth for his distraught mother. He couldn't be the Knight of Swords since he wasn't in the least chivalrous, but she could see him in a uniform and wielding a gun.

With Mrs. Hines and Ossie settled in the large overstuffed chair, Grayce walked to the supply cabinet in the spacious office over-looking the Lake Washington waterway. The view of the water always helped to center her before a treatment.

Taking out the needles for her acupuncture treatment, she breathed deeply to diffuse her nervousness. She recognized her own anxiety when faced with other's hopelessness. She felt driven to try to alleviate the painful grief, but the brother's presence was altering the healing space.

Hunter's direct stare in the reflection of the glass cabinet doors shot spikes of foreboding up her neck. She needed to take control of the churning energy.

She took one last cleansing breath and turned toward the mother who waited for Grayce to perform a miracle. Grayce modulated her voice to the warm, soothing tone she used on agitated animals. "Please, Mr. Hines, there is no need to stand while I treat Ossie." She pulled a chair next to the treatment chair. He moved the chair to the side of the treatment chair to give himself a better angle for watching Grayce work.

She couldn't allow him to distract her from Ossie and her hope to ease Mrs. Hines' pain. She knelt in front of Ossie who was stretched across Mrs. Hines' lap and pitched her voice into a soft lyrical cadence. "You're lovely, my friend. You must be missing Angie."

Tears formed in Mrs. Hines's eyes. Grayce heard Hunter shift in his chair. She took another deep breath and ignored the intense resistance and threat exuding from Hunter Hines. She concentrated on Ossie. The cat's only response to Grayce's presence was a blink of her unfathomable bright green eyes.

Grayce ran her hand several inches above Ossie's back, evaluating the energy along the cat's spine. Her hand slowed over the lung points. She wasn't surprised by the intense heat radiating over the center of emotion. She kept her hand steady and absorbed the energy of the sticky lung points. Ossie needed treatment for the reactive lung points and balancing of her kidney and spleen points.

Grayce slowed her mind and, breathing to connect to her deep quiet space, placed the first thin filiform needle into the crown of Ossie's head. A burst of heat shot through the needle into her hand and a shadow floated in the periphery of her vision. Ignoring the moving blackness creeping closer, she focused on Ossie's treatment. The excessive heat was a symptom of Ossie's stagnant chi.

Grayce moved to treat the sticky lung points. With placement of the needle, the shadows in the periphery crowded and narrowed her vision. An incessant throb began behind her eyes. She closed her eyes for a brief second to stop the pain and the rolling shadows. She drifted in a sea of dark bleakness until she heard a man's voice.

She opened her eyes to find Hunter Hines standing over her. "Quite a show, Dr. Walters."

Disoriented with an agonizing headache, Grayce stared up at the aggressive man.

"I apologize." She didn't know what had happened to her, but she refused to explain.

She ignored Hunter and consciously visualized a ball of incandescent light exploding like a fiery comet into the healing space. One part of her brain registered the fact that the shimmering ball resembled Aunt Aideen's crystal ball. She'd think about the implications later. She refocused on the bright light shooting from the ball and then imagined the lightness spreading into her hands and into the needles in Ossie's body.

With placement of the needles down Ossie's back, the spotted cat went into a deep, calm sleep.

Grayce rotated the needles, sending healing light and harmony toward Ossie.

Grayce leaned back on her heels after finishing the treatment. Her head ached. She rarely got headaches and never during a treatment. She tried to reconcile her headache and the dark lights with the treatment. Ossie's chi wasn't depleted, which would indicate despair or deep grief, and that made her hopeful that Angie wasn't dead. But what had caused her headache? Dr. Z, her mentor, had said her abilities were expanding. Maybe they were expanding her brain against her cranium.

Mrs. Hines whispered as Ossie slept on, "I can't believe Ossie let you put needles into her head."

"Acupuncture is usually very relaxing."

Mrs. Hines' anticipation and desperation were palpable. "Did you learn anything about Angie?"

Grayce had known this moment would come, but it didn't lessen the discouragement sitting in her stomach. And as she had anticipated, she had nothing to offer about Angie's whereabouts. All she had accomplished was to intensify the older woman's pain and confuse herself.

"I'm sorry. I got nothing specific from Ossie. Nothing that would be useful in your search for Angie."

Hunter stood as if ready to leave. "Why am I not surprised?" His derisive voice darted through the silence.

She stood and faced the towering man. "I don't think we should give up yet." She looked down on the seated woman and cat. "From my treatment, I perceived that Ossie is upset by Angie's disappearance, but what gives me hope is that Ossie isn't deeply grieving. There is always an induced stress which is hard to differentiate from grief when an animal comes into a strange office."

Grayce ventured a look at Hunter. He hadn't changed his

soldier's ramrod posture or his pinpoint glare. "I'd like to treat Ossie in her own space. I might be able to detect something more."

"What?" Hunter's bass voice echoed in the large room.

Grayce wouldn't be deterred by one antagonistic man, not after prevailing against an arsonist and a murderer. She ignored Hunter's outrage and spoke to Mrs. Hines. "I can't promise you anything. But I'd like to treat Ossie once more before giving up."

The older woman stared up at her son. Grayce heard her quiet plea. "Please." He took a moment before he nodded at his mother. No words of comfort, no solace offered to his grieving mother.

When Mrs. Hines and Ossie left the room to make their appointment, Hunter turned back toward Grayce, his voice low and menacing, "I don't know what game you're playing, but stay out of my way."

Grayce flopped into her chair after the Hines's departure. She wished her offer to treat Ossie had been lead only by her compassion for the grieving mother. But anger and suspicion about Hunter Hines and the need to prove him wrong had pushed her into an impulsive plan. How was she going to discover anything different about the grieving cat in Angie's apartment? Unlike Mrs. Hines, she knew she was no psychic.

CHAPTER FIVE

Hot, bubbling water swirled around Grayce's feet. The eucalyptus salts didn't mask the harsh smell of the acrylic chemicals in the tiny nail salon on Broadway. Grayce leaned back into the faux leather massage chair and tried to release the lingering tension from last night's dreams.

A smirking Hunter Hines changed into the Knight of Swords and chased her through dark alleyways in Pioneer Square like her real chase by the Russian mob. She wanted to believe it was an anxiety dream, but she knew it was a premonition of coming danger.

James, seated in the massage chair next to Grayce, showed the tiny Vietnamese woman a bottle of white nail polish. "What do you think, Lon?"

Lon stopped scrubbing the bottoms of his feet. She nodded and said in a soft voice, "Very nice."

James and Grayce always requested Lon and tipped her generously after they had heard her life story. Lon had fled Vietnam and an abusive husband. She now lived in White Center and rode two buses to get to her job. Her salon earnings supported her and her two children.

James showed Grayce his color choice—a pearly white.

"White toenails? A little sedate for Gay Bingo," Grayce said.

Both had been a bit too unusual for the their high school scene in their elite school, and as under dogs often do, she and James had bonded in their 10th grade chemistry class. They had remained close friends ever since.

Grayce and James were the only ones in the salon so late in the day. Tucked behind two fake Ficus trees, they had a sense of total privacy.

"White and virginal to match my incredible ensemble, a white satin peignoir and slip of lace around my shoulders—Grace Kelly in her seduction scene in *Rear Window.*"

The memory of their Friday movie nights and their love of film noir, the black and white films of the 40s and 50s, coalesced into a warm reassurance, lifting the dread from her nightmare.

"Remember when Jimmy Stewart asked Grayce Kelly what she had in the little suitcase? How many times have we watched *Rear Window?*" Grayce asked.

"Not as many times as The Lady Vanishes or The 39 Steps."

Grayce didn't share James' obsession with Grace Kelly, Audrey Hepburn or vintage clothing, but she and James both fantasized about playing one of the gutsy, cool, blondes in the Hitchcock movies.

"I'm going to carry a 50's make-up case. And wait 'til you see the blond wig Tony Tequila did for me," James said.

"Will people get that you're Grace Kelly?"

"Honey, are you kidding? This is a ballroom filled with queens."

"What's Tony wearing?"

"Madonna in a black bustier and fishnet stockings. I tried to warn him that he'll be *so* outdated. The room will be filled with Lady Gagas and Beyoncés. Besides, nobody wants to be reminded of the 80's. But Tony remains obsessed with Madonna."

"What's the theme for the soiree?"

James fluttered his long eyelashes. It was unfair that James had thick, black eyelashes that matched his dark, wavy hair and black eyes. "Racy and Lacey. And I'm not leaving Gay Bingo this time no matter how frantic your phone call."

"You loved coming out in drag and playing the damsel in distress," Grayce said.

James combed his fingers through his perfectly coiffed hair then threw his head back in his very practiced affectation. "Honey, I won't risk my peignoir to save your boyfriend's ass this time."

"You won't have to rush out of Gay Bingo. We're going to the Mariner's game."

James' face twisted in merriment, trying hard not to laugh. "But... but...you hate sporting events." His dark eyes danced. "Oh, my God. It must be love."

"It's Davis' first season without his dad. He couldn't go last year. It's going to be a tough night for Davis." Grayce sat back in the chair and breathed deeply of the eucalyptus.

"And you'll be his support."

Grayce shrugged. "Well I suppose that's true."

James winked. "Yes. His supportive supporter. His athletic supporter—you might say."

"Don't get fresh, princess." Grayce shot back.

James stretched languidly as Lon buffed the toes on his left foot. "Perish the thought honey—this one's every inch a queen."

Besides their shared quirkiness, Grayce and James also shared traumatic losses at a young age. In high school, Grayce's sister had died in a car accident and James' mother had succumbed to breast cancer.

James lost his affectation and became serious. "I understand where Davis is coming from. I hated going into Fredrick and Nelson after my mom died. I'd tear up every time I walked into the store. The smell of Estee Lauder perfume at the front door would bring back all the memories of my mom, shopping in her fur coat with her Chanel bag."

Grayce squeezed his arm. Her friendship with James had saved her when her adolescent world had fallen apart.

"Still doesn't explain why you're going to an event with a shouting mass of drunk people," James said.

"Thanks for making it sound like so much fun. Davis could've taken one of his sisters or brothers-in-law, but he asked me. I couldn't say no."

"Honey, this is Uncle Jamesie. You can tell me the truth."

"I want to go."

"Liar, liar, pants on fire," James rhymed.

Grayce punched James' arm. "Very funny."

"But you hate loud noises and crowds."

"I don't hate them. The noise and energy levels are somewhat overwhelming."

"Blend, have a beer, eat a dog...I mean a hot dog."

"I knew what you meant. And for your information, *homie,* I can blend. I just don't want Davis to be disappointed that I'm not into baseball. His ex was a total sports fanatic."

"Yeah, and Daphne slept with his best friend."

Grayce winced. James wasn't known for subtlety.

"Honey, he gets who you are. He doesn't care if you like baseball." James faked a cough behind his hand. "Hard to imagine that handsome hulk wanting you over me."

Grayce was tired from her nightmares and couldn't enjoy James' banter. She understood at a level that couldn't be explained that her involvement with the Hineses was taking her down a dangerous path.

James, sensitive to the change in Grayce's mood, asked, "How was your visit with the missing woman's cat?"

Grayce shook her head. If she couldn't tell James, her best friend, about the overwhelming awareness that she needed to find the missing woman, how could she explain it to Davis? After her involvement in Davis' arson case, she had promised never again to venture into criminal investigations.

James leaned sideways in his chair to get a better angle. He slowly scrutinized Grayce's face. "You're not telling me something."

"I'm going to the missing woman's apartment."

"What?" James sat up quickly and inadvertently lifted his feet out of the water. "Sorry, Lon. I got excited." The slight woman eased James' foot back into the pedicure bath.

"I don't understand. You let that reporter browbeat you into seeing these people, and now you're going to the apartment?"

"I know." Grayce sat back in her chair and hit the neck and back massage button. "But something's not right about the whole situation."

"You got that from the cat?" James asked.

In a rare moment, James wasn't joking about her ability to communicate with animals.

"Ossie is a beautiful, sweet cat, but I didn't learn anything about Angie's whereabouts."

"You better not let Napoleon hear you talk about Ossie in glowing terms."

"It wasn't the cat, it was Angie's brother. I don't trust him." She wasn't exaggerating that she didn't trust Hunter Hines. Her intuition went into high alert around him. She needed time with Hunter Hines to assess whether or not he posed a threat before she confided her suspicions to James or Davis.

"The brother? Maybe you picked up on his frustration at not being able to find his sister."

"No, I don't think so." She didn't know if Aunt Aideen had influenced her perceptions about the tall, dark stranger or not, but she aimed to find out.

"Why? What's he like?"

"Tall, dark, brooding..."

"God, he sounds perfect."

"Not likely into men who dress as Grace Kelly."

"You'd be surprised." James arched one of his carefully shaped eyebrows. "The appearance of a tall, dark, brooding stranger. Time to check your horoscope."

A strange uneasiness flashed through Grayce. Although James was joking, he was getting too close to Aunt Aideen's prediction. She wasn't ready to tell James about her evening with Aunt Aideen since she knew the prediction was true. James wouldn't be able to control the endless jokes about the crystal ball, incense and moonstone.

"Hunter Hines was skeptical about the acupuncture treatment. He made it quite clear that he only tolerated the visit for his mother's sake. And he wasn't nice to his mom. And she's a sweet woman. I want to help her."

James rolled his eyes toward the ceiling. He definitely had mastered the diva eye-rolling better than Hollie. "Here we go again. Grayce, you can't fix everyone's problems."

"I had hoped I could bring some comfort to Angie's mom."

James gave a loud, dramatic sigh. "Sweetie, this isn't your problem. What can you do for Angie's mom? She knows her daughter with PTSD is out wandering the streets of Seattle."

"Exactly, my point. Who is going to help her?" Grayce understood, at some level, that her need to help Angie's mom was related to her inability to help her own mom after her sister's death. She had to trust her deep instinct that she was meant to help Angie's mom.

"Didn't you hear a word I said?"

Grayce leaned forward, inspecting Lon's work on James' toes. "The white looks great."

"I won't say anything else. But don't forget, I tried to warn you. Now tell me more about the suspicious brother. He sounds delicious."

Grayce turned toward James and recited, "Distrustful, serious demeanor, disciplined."

"He sounds like Davis."

"No, he's nothing like Davis. Hunter is cold and clinical. He didn't show any brotherly concern for his missing sister."

"God, are you saying you think he's responsible?"

"No, of course not." Grayce's foot jerked when Lon scrubbed with the loofa. Grayce's hands and feet were very sensitive to touch.

"Are you sure you're not reacting because he didn't appreciate your talents?"

It was more than his disapproval that caused her misgivings about Hunter Hines. "It's hard when someone responds that I'm a quack."

"He said that?"

"No, it was the way he looked at me during the treatment. He's rigid."

"Rigid. I like a man..."

"Don't go there, James."

"I'd like to be a fly on the wall when you tell Davis about the handsome brother."

She had a pretty clear vision of how Davis, who had already decided not to like Hunter Hines, was going to react to her further involvement. "What color for me? I was thinking something dramatic, maybe even red?"

James laughed again.

"What?" She didn't mean to sound impatient, but she hated when her friend understood her too well.

"Nice try. I think you should do the red...but back to the more interesting tidbit. What are you going to tell Davis?"

Davis definitely would understand her compassion for Angie's mother, but he definitely wouldn't understand her need for further association with the missing woman's brother or the connection between his aunt's prediction and Hunter Hines.

"I don't want to ruin the baseball game. I'll tell him after."

"Coward."

Was James right? Was she a coward? This relationship stuff wasn't easy. Being single, she was used to making her own decisions, following her intuition. "Since I've never been to a baseball game, what should I wear?"

"You haven't fooled me by switching to my favorite topic. Although your relationship with the hot fire investigator is in my top picks of juicy discussions."

James sat back and inspected her blue jeans, t-shirt and ponytail. "Wear your usual..." He coughed into his hand as if it was difficult for him to speak. "Style." Grayce's disinterest in fashion was an ongoing debate between the friends.

"I don't always wear blue jeans."

"Really?"

"Okay. I do. They don't take any thought."

"Why don't you let Uncle Jamesie help you shop?"

"What do you have in mind?"

James rubbed his chin back and forth as if contemplating a serious crime. "You won't have to worry about getting cold in Safeco Field since my idea will definitely warm things up between you and Davis. He'll be in a great mood to hear about your next rescue mission."

"I'm not going to wear anything outrageous."

"Outrageous? When have you seen me wear outrageous?"

This from the man dressing as Grace Kelly. But James had sophisticated taste and always looked as if he'd stepped out of *GQ* magazine. He read both men and women's fashion magazines. *Vogue*, *Elle*. French *Vogue*. The list went on.

"You have fabulous taste," she said.

"Since I'm in a Grace Kelly kind of mood. I think we should start with Castaner espadrilles. Grace Kelly made his espadrilles into icons. Do you remember the great 50s black and white shot with Grace and Castaner? Oh, God, I'll have to buy a pair, too."

"I'd love to have new sandals."

"You can't call Castaner espadrilles sandals. They are much more than sandals. I predict it's going to get blazing hot at Safeco Field when Davis sees you in the sexy Castaners."

Everyone seemed to be in the mood to make predictions about Grayce's life this week. She agreed with James that it was going to get hot in Safeco Field—not from her sexy espadrilles, but from Davis' blistering reaction to her involvement in a dangerous case.

CHAPTER SIX

A hot summer night—perfect for Mariners baseball. Davis gazed over at the empty seat and swallowed against the feelings tightening his throat. These were the same seats he and his dad had shared for years of cold, rainy baseball seasons. His dad should have been here, awaiting Felix Hernandez's first pitch.

He needed his dad tonight. His dad would be a great sounding board as he debated the tough choice he faced. The chief had promoted him to captain, but also offered Davis the chance to work on the national level in Washington DC. After the wharf fire, he realized how much satisfaction he got from solving serious crimes, not just arson. This move was a chance to assess his next career step. There was only one problem with his making his next career decision. He had to leave Grayce for six months.

Davis kept scanning the crowd for Grayce as the stadium filled. She had been detained in her office to take care of a yellow lab that had indulged in an overdose of chocolate.

He watched Hernandez go through his warm up. Armed with his wicked split finger fastball, Hernandez had the mojo to go up against tonight's strong Red Sox batting order. The pitcher's predictable ritual of rubbing down the ball with both hands, smoothing the mound with his right foot, didn't bring the usual comfort. For Davis, the familiar rituals of baseball were fused with loss.

"Davis, what great seats." Grayce scrambled over the men in the aisle to get to the center.

What the hell was she wearing? His dad's cronies, the old lechers, were watching her sashay toward the middle seat in her short shorts and a tight top showcasing her snug yoga body.

He was suddenly hot and irritated. What was she thinking wearing that outfit? Where were her usual blue jeans? And her ponytail? She had pinned her dazzling blonde hair on top of her head and little wisps of hair clung to her graceful neck. Davis took a deep breath. He was in shorts and a t-shirt, but hell, he looked nothing like luscious Grayce.

"Davis, what's the matter?" Grayce slipped into the seat next to him. She had no clue that she had just heated the entire male fan section.

He pulled her close and pressed a hard, possessive kiss to her lips.

Shouts came from behind. "Davis, you're killin' us man."

There were more hoots and loud laughs. He knew what was on the men's minds; the same thing that rampaged through his body. Grayce's face turned red, either from the heat or his demanding kiss.

Her green eyes were rounded in surprise. "I'm glad to see you, too."

"How's your patient?" His voice was gruff.

"Recovering. Gus ate half of a Martha Stewart chocolate ganache cake. He had a few tremors, nothing like Mitzi."

"Mitzi was poisoned." He still couldn't believe that bastard had come after his dog during his last investigation.

He looked down at Grayce. His height gave him full view of Grayce's cleavage. His mind drifted away from criminals.

"Davis, your face is bright red. Is this heat bothering you?"

It took all his control not to comment that it was her exposed body causing the blood to flow in hot rushes through his body. He had learned early from his sisters never to criticize what a woman wore. Never. He was struggling to find a happy balance, somewhere between frustration and lust.

"Do you like my new shoes?" Grayce stretched out her toned leg. "They're called espadrilles. James talked me into them."

Davis admired her finely shaped leg. Her shoes tied with a ribbon that wrapped around her delicate ankle. He wanted to untie that ribbon. He took a deep breath, trying not to betray his rapid breathing. How could a woman's shoe affect him this much? Damn James. It was just like him to find the sexiest shoes.

The blood thundered in his head. Oblivious to his friends and the game, Davis stood, pretending interest in Felix's position at home plate to give himself time to control his need to ravish Grayce. Grayce stood when he did. She pressed her warm woman's body against his side. He was in trouble.

"Man, Davis, down!"

Davis and Grayce both sat.

"Do you know everyone in this section?" Grayce asked.

"Just the ones you're driving crazy."

"What?"

"Your outfit...men like that kind of outfit. And your shoes are..."

Grayce looked at him. "My outfit? I'm in shorts and tank top... just like every other woman here."

Davis ran his hand along her toned thigh. "But you don't look like every woman here. You look...you look so damn perfect." He wrapped his arm around her and pulled her closer. "You make me forget I'm at a baseball game. You make me want to go home." He controlled his urge to run his fingers along the edge of her tight top.

"What? And miss Felix Hernandez's splitter?"

Davis jerked his head up. "What did you say?"

He had been sure Grayce had never been to a Mariners game. He had assumed she barely knew about the elementary rules of balls and strikes.

She laughed out loud, and her incredible, soft, curvaceous body shook with delight to have surprised him. Like a big buffoon, he couldn't stop smiling at her enjoyment. He kept smiling, knowing at that moment, he would never let Grayce Walters go. He'd do anything to keep her in his life. He'd fly home every weekend from DC.

"Davis, the shock on your face was worth all the research."

"I expected you wouldn't know anything about baseball."

"I don't, but the Internet makes any subject easy to research."

"You researched baseball on the web?"

"I did. And I'm excited to see a hundred-mile-an-hour ball aimed at the batter's head." His nurturing, tender woman sounded blood-thirsty.

"I can't believe this is your first game."

"My dad isn't a big sports fan. He plays tennis and golf. That's about it."

"My dad and I sat in these seats all my years of growing up. The story my sisters like to tell is that my dad wanted to start bringing me when I was two, but my mom made him hold off 'til four. My dad agreed only because of the diapers. And then we never stopped."

Grayce got a wistful look on her face. He knew she was imagining him as a boy with his dad. And he too was remembering. He got a lump in his throat that wouldn't move.

She reached for his hand, lacing her fingers between his. "What wonderful memories you have with your dad."

Grayce somehow made painful things become lighter. After two years, he was beginning to remember and appreciate the moments with his dad. Her small hand pressed against his, eased the pain.

"What else did you learn about baseball?"

"Baseball fans love to quantify everything. I enjoyed the comparison of stats. Did you know how much more important ERA is than wins or strike-outs per game?"

Now it was his turn to laugh out loud. Grayce was a quick study, and listening to her understanding of baseball stats, he realized how quickly she had come to understand the game. His male domain was being invaded by this spunky little woman with the wondrous body and sharp mind—and it didn't bother him one bit.

The crowd erupted. The much anticipated Felix Hernandez was taking the mound. The neon board flashed. Shouts of "Ole" and Mariachi music filled the stadium. Everyone was on their feet.

Grayce pulled on his hand to lean down. She yelled in the midst of the noise, "I'm afraid with the speed of the pitch I won't be able to tell the balls from strikes."

He bent close to her ear. "Watch where the ball comes over the plate."

She looked up at him. "I'll try."

He couldn't resist her or her earnestness. He had to kiss her again. He molded his lips against her soft mouth. "I like you at the game."

Her eyes had softened, and her voice got raspy. "I like being here."

They were interrupted when Hernandez threw a chest high fast-ball for a strike.

"Did you see how the ball blew by him?"

Grayce nodded. Her eyes remained riveted on Hernandez.

The stocky ace pulled at the brim of his cap and then resumed his focus on the target from the catcher. With one wicked splitter, Hernandez ended the inning. The crowd cheered wildly. People began to stream into the aisles in search of beer and food. Grayce and Davis stood to stretch.

"Davis, I'm gonna go get some food. I'm starving. What do you want?"

He immediately visualized Grayce climbing the stairs in her shorts and wandering through the hordes of randy male fans.

"I'll go with you."

"You don't want to miss the beginning of the next inning."

He took her arm and whispered into her ear. "I'm coming. Every man here is going to want to jump you, dressed in that sexy outfit."

"Right." She rolled her eyes. She thought he was joking. "Davis, I'm sure at least half of the men are too interested in the game to even notice."

"Not notice. Are you kidding? They'd have to be dead not to appreciate your...your beauty." He stared at her cleavage.

Grayce sat back down. "I'm wearing exactly what all the other women are wearing. Why are you upset?"

"I don't like the idea of other men seeing you in those shorts...and that top. I want you all to myself." He looked at the way the tank top was molded to her firm breasts. The heat surged through his body. "Honey, let's go to my place." He caressed her warm thigh. "It's been two nights."

"I know." Her voice sounded breathless. Or maybe it was his. Grayce ran her finger over his roving hand. "But what about the game? What about Hernandez?"

"Who?" His finger was wandering higher on her hot flesh. He liked making her face flush.

He was having trouble not panting. "We can watch the game and eat at my place."

"Are you sure you want to leave the game?"

He couldn't keep the heat out of his voice. "I'm definitely sure."

CHAPTER SEVEN

D avis' heart boomed against his chest and his breaths came in fierce surges as he and Grayce ascended in the elevator. He was a hair's breath away from taking her in the glass elevator. Did Grayce realize her peril? She leaned into him but remained silent. His harsh breathing was the only sound in the empty elevator.

He had to control his body for only a few more minutes. He'd unlock his condo door, then he'd remove Grayce's clothes then his, and then he'd act out every fantasy he'd had since Grayce sashayed into the Mariners game.

Grayce's earthy scent filled his nostrils and when he looked down at her generous, womanly curves in her tight top, he knew he was fighting a losing battle. The primal need to touch her was winning.

He only intended to kiss her, but when she wrapped her arms around his neck and used the tip of her tongue to outline his lips, he was lost. His tongue swept into her mouth, stroking her. He savored the taste of her.

She melted against him. He felt her surrender all through his body, and a ferocious, male exultation swept through him. She was completely his. No one else could have her. After a long drugging kiss to let her know that she belonged to him, he finally got around to stepping out of the elevator.

With Grayce barely a few steps into his condo, he pressed her against the wall. He slammed the door closed with his foot. He twisted her hair around his fist, forced her head back. He growled. "Now, you're going to pay for wearing that top."

Grayce gave a low, husky laugh that went straight to his groin.

In one quick movement, he pulled the top off, exposing her lush breasts. He lifted her full breasts to his mouth. "I've been wanting to do this since you arrived at the game." He lowered his lips to a succulent breast. He circled his tongue around the nipple then did the same to her other breast. With lips, tongue, and hands, he branded her as his woman.

Grayce was writhing against the wall.

"I want you as hot and bothered as I've been."

Grayce wound her fingers into his hair and pushed her breast against his mouth. His gentle healer was a passionate woman.

"Is this what you want?" He trailed his tongue around her firm soft breast as he squeezed.

Grayce's moans of pleasure fired his hunger.

"And for wearing these shorts, I'm going to make you scream my name."

He unbuttoned her shorts and slowly pulled them down her legs. Grayce had on a lacy thong. He had never seen her in a thong. If he had known what she was wearing under her shorts, he would never had made it home.

"A thong?" His voice came out half needing, half pleading. "You never wear a thong."

"With white shorts, I didn't want my panties to show through."

"Grayce, you're killing me." His finger traced the back of the thong in the warm, moist crevice of her voluptuous ass. He panted as if he had sprinted up all twenty-five floors to his condo. He quickly dispensed of her thong. A nude Grayce, backed against the wall in her sexy shoes, made him lose total control.

"I'm sorry, Grayce, I meant to go slow," he rasped as he stripped out of his clothes in less than five seconds.

"I don't want you to go slow." Her voice, husky with desire, needing him, shot flames of heat down his spine.

He lifted her up and slowly slid her onto his erection. She was tight and hot. She cried out his name when he brought himself fully into her.

"Wrap your legs around me." The heels of her shoes dug into his back, making him wild. "Just like that," he groaned.

He lifted her and thrust deeply to make the possession complete. He was embedded in his sweet woman. She clung to his driving body. With the hoarse sounds she made against his throat, she set his blood on fire.

He brought her close to climax, then deliberately delayed her pleasure. "You're mine, Grayce Walters. Only mine. Tell me."

He stilled and took her breast into her mouth, suckling hard.

"I'm yours, Davis. Always yours."

Her words unleashed all his passion and need to please her. He thrust deeper, fusing their bodies with his penetration.

On the edge, she dug her heels deeper into his back and arched in his arms. Her movement made him lose his last remnant of control. He couldn't slow down, pounding into Grayce, he brought them to shuddering, mindless frenzy until there was nothing but themselves.

Davis was stretched on his back with his arm wrapped around Grayce. Her fingers wandered on his chest. "I can't believe we left the game. All that research on baseball, and I only saw one inning."

She caressed his abdomen. He took a deep breath. He couldn't believe how many times they had made love since arriving home.

His fingers began their own wandering, inching toward a rosy pink nipple. "This is a lot better than baseball."

He hadn't given a thought to baseball since Grayce had pranced into Safeco Field. He had left opening night with Felix Hernandez pitching.

"What is it, Davis? Did I just hear a sigh?"

"No. It's just...I've never left a game before it was finished."

Grayce sat up and stared into his eyes. Her vibrant hair cascaded down her back and hung in front of her eyes.

She pushed the hair away from her face and leaned closer to him, her soft breasts rubbed against his chest. "Do you regret leaving?"

"Hell, no." He started to pull on her wrist.

"But there was a sigh. I heard it."

He wasn't sure if he had really sighed, but Grayce seemed to be able to understand his feelings better than he did. Her eyes widened as she searched his face.

Had his behavior tonight shocked her? It had shocked him. He didn't think Grayce would appreciate his male, territorial thoughts and his need to claim and possess her, to make sure she understood she belonged to him, only him. All he could think about was taking Grayce home and making her his own. He hadn't cared about the Mariners or Felix Hernandez.

"Davis, I'm happy to go back to the game, if that's what you want."

God, was she insane? He was getting aroused again by her hot thigh draped across his and the soft breast that he could easily take into his mouth.

"I'm very happy right where I am."

"But you and your dad never left a game."

His dad would've agreed that loving Grayce was the right choice for tonight and every night. "My dad would understand. I'm sorry that he didn't get to meet you. He would've loved you."

He had stopped himself from saying "like I love you." Grayce wasn't ready for a declaration of love. Her sister's death had deeply affected her. She was afraid to get too close to anyone for fear of losing them. Plucky Grayce wouldn't appreciate his interpretation.

When they had discussed their wariness in rushing a commitment in their first month of dating, he hadn't been totally truthful. His feelings would overwhelm Grayce. Hell, they overwhelmed him. He had never been in love before, and now he had to leave Seattle. He wasn't sure how to tell Grayce about the promotion.

Grayce was very intuitive; she must know how crazy he was about her, something was wrong. He cursed himself for not having the courage to come clean tonight. But then those perky little shorts came off, and he lost his train of thought.

CHAPTER EIGHT

Dressed in Davis' t-shirt, Grayce sat cross-legged at the dining room table. Mitzi waited under the table, hoping to catch any dropped food. Grayce had lost interest in the food on her plate. The evening had been wonderful until Davis had announced he needed to discuss something serious. The demanding, passionate, and tender man of the last hours had transformed into a somber, resolute man about to face the gallows.

Anxiety churned in Grayce's stomach. "It's about your Aunt Aideen, isn't it?" She pushed her plate away.

"My aunt? Why would I want to talk about my aunt?"

Grayce lightly exhaled. Aunt Aideen hadn't shared the prediction with him.

"You're looking so serious." His shoulders were tightened, and the little laugh lines that she loved had flattened.

"In my meeting with the chief..." He pulled his chair closer to hers so their knees touched. He took her hand into his and pressed a hot, moist kiss against her palm. Davis' eyes blazed with need—the look that always made her stomach flutter.

"I haven't told you all the news. The chief recommended me to be the department's liaison at the Fusion Center." Davis delivered the information in a fatal tone.

"Sounds like it's an honor. Why aren't you pleased?"

He continued to hold her hand, rubbing his thumb on the inside of her palm. It would've been a sensual experience except Davis was distracted and didn't seem to realize he was touching her.

"What is the Fusion Center?" She asked.

"King County's joint task force on terrorism. The center is a unified command where all the agencies come together to assess credible threats. It's under the umbrella of the Department of Homeland Security."

"Terrorist threats in the Northwest?" The little hairs on Grayce's arms and neck stirred and her intuition flared. She repressed the worry that Davis could be in danger.

"It's a big deal. The chief was impressed with my ability to work with all the different agencies during the wharf fire investigation. He liked the way I handled the Feds and prevented the investigation from becoming a pissing match."

"How wonderful and well-deserved. I know you really enjoyed the collaboration with the federal agencies."

His bright eyes suddenly became inscrutable. "Exactly. I found the FBI and the DEA's work intriguing."

Grayce waited, suspended as if Davis were a lawyer, developing his argument before delivering the lethal accusation.

"It sounds great. You'll work more closely with the Feds, right?" She grabbed his hand. "Why aren't you happy?"

"I'll definitely have more time in the Federal arena." He laughed in a deprecating voice she had never heard before.

"Honey, you know how much I care about you. Nothing will ever change that." His voice and his bright eyes were ardent with feelings.

This was worse than she thought. Grayce's heart thumped against her chest. Why the testimonial about his feelings?

"The chief has recommended me for a very select training

program..." Davis paused. His eyes didn't meet hers but stared behind her.

Mitzi arose from beneath the table and sat next to Grayce in her protective stance.

Grayce shifted in her chair. The timber in his voice changed when he said "select training program." She felt his eager interest.

Davis had last changed careers when he moved home to take care of his dying father. He left the world of investment banking resolved to find meaningful work. With his multiple talents and drive, Grayce wasn't sure how long he'd remain a fire investigator.

"Grayce, three months ago, I'd be jumping at this opportunity but now..."

"I don't understand. What's stopping you from this training?"

"You...us. I can't leave now."

"Leave? You said the Fusion Center is in King County."

"The National Center, honey—Washington, DC."

"DC? You can't be serious?" Her voice came out as a high-pitched screech.

"The chief wants me to go to DC. He wants me to represent the department on the national level."

Grayce felt as if someone had flipped her onto her back in Aikido training. Her breath was knocked out and the room spun.

She sat upright in the chair. Her feet now on the ground. "How long is the training for?"

"At least six months, but the chief wants me to stay for twelve months."

Grayce wasn't sure if she could speak, since she couldn't draw air into her lungs. Davis not in Seattle. Her mind was in shock. She was tempted to act like a needy woman in a bad romance and beg him not to leave.

"This is a great opportunity for you, Davis." She tried to sound convincing. It was absolutely the right thing to say.

"I told the chief I'd need time to talk with you before deciding."

"It sounds like the perfect next step." She heard the words in her own ears as if someone else was speaking.

"It's a long time for me to be away from you. Won't it feel like that for you, too?"

She leaned toward him and ran her hand up his arm, needing to touch him, to make the raw pain in her chest vanish. She had started to believe that she and Davis could make it work and now he was leaving. "Of course it will be a long time to go without you, but I want what's best for you." Her words were sincere, but it would take her heart a while to believe them.

"But you're the best for me, Grayce."

She ignored the queasy feeling in her stomach. "Davis, I can't go to DC."

"I wouldn't want you to give up your practice. I know what it means to you."

Grayce felt relieved and terribly disappointed.

"I know we agreed that we wouldn't push our relationship and we'd take it nice and slow." He stared at her with wary longing. "The possibility of you meeting someone else while I'm gone... it's why I went a little crazy at the game."

His past betrayals were rearing their head. They both had demons around trust and commitments—major hurdles for a long-time relationship.

"Why would you think that I'd want to go out with someone else?"

"People break promises. I speak from experience."

"I wouldn't make a promise I couldn't keep."

"I know you're not like that, but you'll be meeting men, and I'll be gone. Hell, when I was in your office, you were about to meet another man." He started to run his fingers through his hair and then stopped.

"Davis, we're going to have to trust each other."

"I want to be fair to you, Grayce, and think of what's best for you, but I can only think about what's best for me." He stopped himself. "And it's you and the chance to work on the national level."

"I could never stop you from this opportunity. You're ready for the next challenge."

He ran his hand through his hair, making black spikes stand up. "I'm going to hate being separated from you."

"We need to support each other to do the things we really want to do. We can get through this. I've wanted to visit Louise Marley. I'll go to LA when you're gone."

"And meet some handsome Hollywood actor."

"Now you're starting to talk about James' dream. Not mine."

"Tell me your dreams... What you want, Grayce?"

"I have to be lying down on a bed to think about my dreams." She stood and swayed her hips the seductive way that made Davis go insane, or at least that's how he described his feelings. There was only so much talking one could do about trust and commitment. Davis was a very physical man. He'd understand how she felt if she showed him. She pulled off her t-shirt when she got to the door.

CHAPTER NINE

The little hairs on Grayce's neck and arms tingled in heightened awareness as she climbed the rickety stairs to the second floor of the shabby apartment. The 1-5 freeway roared below the 1950's building perched on the edge of Beacon Hill.

Grayce peered over the unsteady railing, expecting to find a pursuer lurking underneath the stairwell. There was nothing threatening below except overgrown blackberry bushes and empty beer cans. Aunt Aideen's predictions and Davis' warnings were making her paranoid.

Grayce knocked on the peeling brown door.

Mrs. Hines answered immediately. "Dr. Walters, we're glad you could come." She gripped Grayce's hands tightly.

The older woman's gray pallor and the slight tick in her left eyelid made it evident that there had been no word of her missing daughter.

Mrs. Hines' lower lip trembled. "Nothing..."

The woman's hopeless exhaustion seeped into Grayce. She

squeezed Mrs. Hines' cold hands. "I'm sorry. The waiting must be terrible."

The woman barely nodded her bowed head. "Come in, please."

Angie's townhouse was sterile with sparse furnishings, bereft of joy and smelled of cleaning products. The aseptic chlorine smell burned Grayce's nostrils.

Hunter Hines stood strategically at the western window, the unobserved observer. Sunlight surrounded him, obscuring his face and making him larger and broader, like a medieval knight.

She walked toward him with her hand outstretched. "Good morning, Mr. Hines."

He stiffened in surprise and took her hand. "Dr. Walters."

His handshake was strong and controlled. She didn't get any intuitive insight from the brisk contact.

She bent to greet Ossie, but the cat was wrapping her way around Hunter's leg. Ossie rubbed herself against Hunter's perfectly creased black pants and his perfectly shined black shoes. A trail of gray hair followed Ossie's path.

Grayce hadn't observed in her office that Hunter's clothing was military issue. Unless he was some sort of secret intelligence agent, Hollie would be able to research his background.

Mrs. Hines hovered near Grayce. "What can I get you to drink? Coffee, tea, water?"

"Water would be great, thank you."

Relieved to be given a task, Mrs. Hines went into the kitchen.

The snowy peaks of the Olympic Mountains were visible behind Hunter. The small apartment had a spectacular view of the mountains, Puget Sound, and the industrial area of Seattle's south end. It wouldn't be long before developers tore down the dilapidated apartment building and built expensive condos, displacing the low-income residents.

"What a great view," Grayce said.

Hunter Hines didn't turn to look at the view. "Yes."

With Hunter's obvious unwillingness to exchange pleasantries,

Grayce walked into the tiny, outdated kitchen. The refrigerator was scattered with pictures. "This looks exactly like my refrigerator," she said.

Mrs. Hines turned from the cupboard and took a picture from the refrigerator and handed it to Grayce. "This picture is right before Angie left for Afghanistan the first time."

Grayce stared at the young woman on the brink of womanhood in her blue Marine Corp jacket and white sash, smiling back at the camera. Angie resembled her brother with dark hair and eyes, but her youthful enthusiasm was nothing like the detached man in the living room.

Mrs. Hines chose another picture from the refrigerator and handed it to Grayce. Angie stood arm in arm with two other women. All were dressed in full camouflage uniforms with rifles on their shoulders. Their faces were browned with Afghan heat and sand. Angie's youthful vibrancy had disappeared. She stared back at the camera, a vacant look filled with war-weariness.

"That's Angie's commander, Lieutenant Ronda Brown." Mrs. Hines pointed to an older woman who stood in the middle. "She was head of the women's engagement team."

"What is an engagement team?" Grayce asked.

"A small group of female Marines were sent to Afghanistan to communicate with the women and children in the villages since the culture prohibits males from speaking to the women."

"Angie was chosen because of her ability to speak those Afghanistan languages—I can never remember their names." She raised her voice. "What are those again, Hunter?"

Hunter Hines answered from the living room, his voice sounding flat—bored or cautious. "Pashto and Dari."

"Angie was the group's translator?"

"There were native translators, but they wanted Marines talking to the women. Angie didn't tell me a lot, but I got the feeling that the engagement group was supposed to get information about the insurgents, kind of like those spy movies." Mrs. Hines whispered in a conspiratorial tone.

An icy chill shot through Grayce's body. She rubbed her hands along her arms, trying to warm herself in the airless condo.

"Angie was thrilled to be part of the select group of Marines and under the leadership of Lieutenant Brown. She had never had a woman as a commander before that."

The bond between Angie and the older women was evident in the way they stood arm in arm in the picture.

"Angie was only a few feet away when the IED killed Rhonda."

"The Lieutenant was killed?"

Mrs. Hines struggled to speak, tears welled in her eyes. "She had two children."

Grayce touched the woman on the shoulder. "We don't need to talk about this."

"Talking actually helps. Angie never talked about what happened. But after the explosion, Angie couldn't sleep and had terrible nightmares."

"I can't imagine how difficult it was for her." Grayce understood the shock of suddenly, unexpectedly losing someone. But this was, not getting to say goodbye because of an accident or a sudden illness, but because of a calculated act of war. Deliberate killing. War was something Grayce couldn't understand, would never understand, and didn't want to understand. Except perhaps, for its effect on Angie.

"Angie blamed herself for her commander's death."

Grayce understood about blame, too. When catastrophe strikes, you look for a reason in the chaos, something you could've done differently.

"Angie changed so much after Rhonda died. She withdrew into herself, spending her days with Ossie."

"I can't imagine what it's like to be in constant danger."

Mrs. Hines pulled on the sleeve of her pressed denim shirt. "Angie was a gentle child. But the Marines are in her blood. Angie and Hunter's dad was a Marine. Just like..."

Mrs. Hines suddenly stopped talking when Hunter Hines appeared in the doorway.

"Are you ready to start, Dr. Walters?" Hunter's voice was clipped.

"I'm just talking with Dr. Walters, Hunter."

"Once you two are done chatting..." By the penetrating look he gave his mother, it was clear he didn't want his mother talking to Grayce.

"I can start the treatment whenever you like," Grayce said.

"I'll wait in the living room for you to finish your conversation."

"I didn't mean to upset Hunter." Grayce was puzzled by the man' antagonism toward his mother. What did it matter if his mother told her about Angie's experience in Afghanistan?

"Don't you worry about Hunter, it's just his way. You sure you don't want anything but water? You need more ice?" Mrs. Hines opened the freezer door.

"That would be great."

A picture fell to the floor when Mrs. Hines closed the freezer door. Grayce bent and retrieved a picture of a group of laughing women.

"Those are Angie's friends from her PTSD group at the VA—all of them have been to Afghanistan and all of them have PTSD. Angie said the group had saved her."

Grayce stared at the picture of the three women—Angie was in the middle, towering over the two. A heavy, black woman in uniform and a petite blonde stood on either side of Angie. All three were laughing. Nothing in the picture hinted at what each of the women had suffered—was suffering.

"The blond girl is in both pictures," Grayce said.

"That's Maddy. She was part of the engagement team in Afghanistan."

"And she's from the Northwest?"

"She moved around a lot, but I think she grew up here. I always thought she moved back because of her friendship with Angie."

"What does Maddy think about Angie's disappearance?'

"Maddy is the one Angie went to find."

"Angie went to look for her friend and disappeared? How long has Maddy been missing?" Grayce examined Maddy's picture more closely. Maddy was smiling, but there was a brittle fragility in her eyes.

"I don't know exactly. But the VA doctor told me that Angie announced to the group that she was going to look for Maddy. That was the last anyone heard from Angie." Mrs. Hines' hand trembled when she took the ice cube container to the sink.

Grayce's intuition flared. What were the chances of two Marines who served in the same unit in Afghanistan going missing?

"No one was surprised by Maddy not showing up for group. She didn't attend regularly like she was supposed to."

Grayce looked at the picture of the women, hoping for some vision or clue to what had prevented the women from coming home.

"Angie had taken on the role of group leader and seemed to be bouncing back from her own problems. Doctor Dagger said that she was making great strides with her PTSD symptoms, but any trauma could make her symptoms flare up to confuse and overwhelm her." Tears streamed down her cheeks. "I'm so afraid that something really bad happened."

Grayce put her arm around the diminutive woman. "It's all going to work out. I know Angie's okay." Had she spoken her thoughts aloud?

The woman wiped the tears with the back of her sleeve. "You're not really just saying that to make me feel better?"

"I have a strong feeling that Angie's lost." Grayce didn't question her intuition: she sensed Angie wasn't dead.

Mrs. Hines took her hand. "Thank you. A mother would know if... I prayed to the Lord to give me strength. He sent you to me."

Heat moved into Grayce's embarrassed face. She wasn't sure that God had sent her to help Mrs. Hines, but she knew something beyond herself compelled her to help the grieving mother.

The older woman released her hand. "I'm sure Hunter is getting impatient with Ossie badgering him."

"What do you mean?"

"Hunter doesn't like cats. And of course, Ossie knows it."

Grayce laughed. She appreciated the contrary inclinations of cats.

Hunter sat on the small, worn love seat close to the kitchen. Why did Grayce get the feeling that Hunter had listened to everything his mother said? Ossie was nowhere in sight.

"Where's Ossie?" Grayce asked.

Hunter stood impatiently and waved toward the hallway. "She went into Angie's bedroom."

Hunter's erect bearing, his clothing, were definitely military. How had she missed it? When she got back to her office, she would have Hollie do a bit of online research on Hunter Hines.

"I'll go fetch him." Grayce wanted the chance to see Angie's bedroom. The bedroom was as barren as the rest of the apartment—either a reflection of Angie's military discipline or her mother's need to stay busy. The only warmth in the dark room was from Ossie's loud purring, curled up on a wicker chair.

No pictures hung on the wall. A large TV sat precariously on storage boxes. A worn, woebegone stuffed dog, some remnant from childhood Grayce supposed, sat on the tightly tucked bed. Angie's intense isolation resonated in the bleak room.

Neither Mrs. Hines nor Hunter followed Grayce into the bedroom. She could hear Hunter's sharp tone as he said something about Maddy and the engagement team. Mrs. Hines murmured softly in response.

Grayce knelt before the wicker chair to be on the same level as Ossie. "How are you, my beauty?"

She ran her hand along Ossie's back, not touching but assessing the heat from the cat's body. Grayce detected no hot spots or stagnant chi. She spoke in a low lyrical voice. "I know you're missing Angie. We're going to find her for you."

Ossie stood and pawed at a white t-shirt. Cats often found conso-lation in their owner's belongings. Ossie laid down and then flipped on the t-shirt in one fluid motion.

"Is this Angie's t-shirt?" Grayce asked.

Ossie kept repeating the stand and flip. Had she misdiagnosed Ossie? Repetitive, obsessive behaviors were a sign of anxiety. Was Ossie more traumatized than she thought?

Grayce's close presence seemed to agitate the cat. "What is it, Ossie? What's gotten you so upset?"

Ossie stood and looked Grayce straight in the eye, green to green. She meowed in a painful cry, then kneaded the t-shirt, digging her claws into the shirt.

"It's okay, Ossie." Ossie continued to scratch at the t-shirt.

"Do you need me to move the t-shirt?"

Ossie gave a mournful cry.

Grayce gently put her hand under Ossie's body and lifted both cat and shirt together. Ossie gave a loud yowl and released her claws. The shirt fell to the floor. Ossie jumped out of Grayce's arms.

Grayce picked up the shirt. It appeared new, not worn-soft as Grayce had suspected. She stared at the familiar logo—Youth Ministry Teen Feed. Grayce didn't know what the connection was between Angie and the t-shirt, but her intuition was humming. This connection was the first hopeful sign.

Ossie bumped Grayce's leg with her striped head, purring loudly.

"Dr. Walters, what are you doing?"

Grayce startled at the sound of Hunter's harsh voice.

"Just greeting Ossie. She's very attached to Angie's t-shirt. Did Angie volunteer at Teen Feed?"

Hunter crossed the room and grabbed the t-shirt from Grayce's hand. "Where did you find this?"

"Ossie was sleeping on it. Is it important?"

Hunter stared at the shirt. "I don't know."

Grayce watched Hunter turn the t-shirt over, carefully inspecting both sides of the shirt. Hunter Hines was as methodical as an investigator.

"What do you know about Teen Feed, Dr. Walters?"

"It's a program that supports street kids. It's connected with several churches in the community. My parents' church is one of the sponsors. I've volunteered there."

"How convenient."

"Excuse me?"

"Well isn't this a cozy coincidence? Who are you? What's your game?"

Grayce stiffened her spine. What was she being accused of? "I'm trying to help your mom."

Hunter continued to examine her face with his piercing black eyes. She was getting pretty tired of him treating her like a criminal.

Mrs. Hines stood at the bedroom door. "What's the matter, Hunter?"

"Have you seen this t-shirt?" He walked toward his mom with the t-shirt in his hand.

"Yes."

"Why didn't you tell me?"

"I didn't know it was important. Ossie liked to sleep on it. I thought it had Angie's scent." Mrs. Hines stared at her son. "Is it a clue?"

"Was Angie involved with this program? Feeding street kids?" he asked.

Mrs. Hines touched the t-shirt tentatively.

Hunter took an impatient, deep breath.

"Did Angie volunteer there?" he asked again.

"Not that I know of. She never told me about what she did when she wasn't at the VA. I know she did a lot of jogging to keep in shape."

Hunter turned toward Grayce. "Where's this program's office?"

"In the University District, but I don't know if they have an office. When I volunteered, we went at night and cooked in the basement of the church."

Hunter turned toward his mother. "I'm going to see what I can find out. I'll call you later."

He looked over his shoulder from the doorway. "I guess you're finished here, Dr. Walters."

If Hunter Hines believed he could dismiss her that easily, he was going to be disappointed. Angie was in danger, and Grayce was compelled to find her. It was part of her gift. "I can't get used to him rushing in and out like that. He's been so wound up." Mrs. Hines shook her head.

Maybe James was right. Hunter's tightly held control reflected his frustration at the endless waiting.

"I understand, Mrs. Hines. The waiting has been hard for both of you." Grayce took the woman's hands into her own.

"Do you want to give Ossie acupuncture?"

"I don't believe he needs a treatment. You're taking great care of him."

"Do you think the t-shirt might help?" The older woman straightened her blouse, tugging at the hem. "I sure hope this is a lead."

Grayce smiled. "I hope so, too."

Grayce didn't want to raise the woman's expectations. Everyone had t-shirts with logos, but it was no accident that Ossie had given her the shirt. and she was going to find out why.

"People will remember Angie if she volunteered there. It's a small group."

"Maybe Angie was there before she...got lost. Dr. Dagger thinks Angie might've had a bad flashback and got confused. Right now, she might not know who she is." Mrs. Hines' voice broke. "He's the one who talked me into going on TV. He hoped she might recognize me."

"It was very brave of you to go on TV."

"Not really. I'd do anything to find Angie. The idea of her wandering the streets..."

As if sensing the terrible fear in the room, Ossie kneaded her paws on Grayce's shoes.

"Ossie sure likes you. She really isn't friendly."

"I like Ossie." Grayce ran her hand along the exotic cat. "She is beautiful, isn't she?"

"Angie's friend Maddy used to wrap Ossie around her neck and pretend she was an expensive fur piece. The girls would laugh."

"Really, I can't imagine Ossie tolerating the roughhousing."

"Ossie seemed to understand the girls needed laughter in their lives." The bright light showed the harsh lines around Mrs. Hines' eyes and lips.

"It's funny how animals seem to know when people need affection and Maddy sure needed affection."

"Why Maddy?"

"All Angie told me was that Maddy had a troubled home life before she went into the Marines. She used to stay here when things got bad. Better here than, you know, on the street."

"Mrs. Hines, could I borrow the picture of Angie and Maddy? I'd like to show the women's picture to the people I know at Teen Feed. If I get any information, I'll call you and you can share with Hunter."

"I'd appreciate anything you could do."

"I need to get back to my office. But if you need anything, please call me."

As she walked downstairs to the car Grayce reflected that she had wanted to reassure the woman, tell Mrs. Hines that she wasn't going to give up until she found Angie, regardless of her son's feelings. However, Hunter Hines' strong yet simmering emotions felt to Grayce like a Pacific Northwest fault line—ominous and ready to rumble. So she kept quiet about it for the present. There may come a time when confronting Hunter Hines might have to happen—but when it did, she wanted to be prepared and rational, not a bundle of emotions herself—and she would prefer to have company if and when that day came.

CHAPTER TEN

Angie stood on the porch in the hot sun. Panic gripped her by the throat. She remembered nothing. Where was she? She tugged at a piece of yellow tape, and it slithered off the railing.

When she turned back to the door she'd just come through. she caught sight of the condemned sign posted by order of the King County Sheriff's Department. Her breath couldn't make it all the way down and into her lungs.

Impulsively she reached for her back pocket. Her hand expected to touch a lump of—what? Wallet? Nothing there. She felt faint and leaned forward on the porch railing as much as she dared, given the decrepitude of the wood.

She forced herself to stillness. Breath at last reached her vital center. But her mind did not clear. She shook her head to clear it, but that only brought on a spasm of excruciating pain. She turned and looked back into one of the unbroken windows at the back of the house. To her terror, she did not recognize the reflection in the window, it might have been someone on TV, or a ghost. The face looking back at her was that of a stranger. She had no memory of who she was or how she had ended up at this condemned house.

She stood terrified, unable to move. Her heart boomed in her chest.

She had to get out of the sun. She needed water. She walked down the steps, following the sound of the traffic to the front of the house.

She dodged the pedestrians on the busy street. Oblivious, she breathed deeply, inhaling fumes from the cars and buses. The noxious smell stirred a vague memory.

Terror clawed at her. She darted into the street. An angry bus driver blasted his horn as he screeched to a sudden stop. She froze at the piercing blast and squeal.

A bright light flashed... the explosions hammered in her head... an IED. Danger! Frantically, she searched the street for a barrel or backpack or suitcase, something that might contain an explosive devices. *Get to minimum safe distance!*

She had to escape. A place to hide. She needed a place to hide. Too dangerous to be exposed this way. She had to get out of the open.

How long could she last out here 'til the Humvees arrived? The bright lights flashed again. Her heartbeat resounded in her ears. Where were the damn choppers?

Panicked, she ran.

CHAPTER ELEVEN

Grayce huddled in a fetal position in a makeshift bed, a bare, stained mattress on a dank cement floor that stank of sewage. Some grim prison cell a million miles from anything human. Although Grayce knew she was dreaming, she couldn't stop the endless terror. Unrelenting explosions and screaming anguish blasted all around her. Acrid smoke burned her nostrils. A sharp pain stabbed between her eyes.

People and places shifted and transformed as the relentless panic swelled inside her. Grayce now ran under the sweltering heat, ran from a raging fire that threatened to consume her. The blazing fire was close on her heals, close to catching her. Intense heat seared the skin on her back and neck.

The nightmare changed. Hunter Hines, a gun in his hand, hunted her through a *jungle*. The path was narrow and reeked of garbage.

"I'll catch you, bitch. And you'll pay." His maniacal laugh echoed in the dark woods.

Fear forced her to run. She ran to reach the end of the long, winding path, where someone waited for her, someone she cared about was in danger, in mortal danger. Someone who hoped she would come soon.

Grayce struggled to wake herself from the terrifying panic. She was caught in death's grip.

"Grayce, wake up. Grayce." Strong hands rubbed her arms, warming her. "Honey, are you okay? You were shouting at me to run...and something about a gun."

Davis' warm voice softened the sharp edge of her fear. He pulled her into his arms, and she put her head on his hard chest. The steady beat of his heart purged the nightmare's dark demons.

Davis pushed a strand of her hair that hung over her eyes behind her ear, placing open mouthed kisses along her moist hairline. "You're sweating."

"In my dream, I was hot."

"Hot." His voice lowered, huskier. "I like hot."

His erection pushed against her leg.

She trailed her finger down his chest. "Not that kind of hot, I was running from a fire."

"Are you still having nightmares from that night? Tell me. Every time I think of that bastard..."

She hadn't meant to get Davis all riled up about their last case. In her half-awake state, she hadn't guarded her words. "No, this dream is most likely from my treatment of Ossie, Angie's cat." She didn't include that the nightmare had possibly come from Aunt Aideen's prediction nor that she had been having recurrent nightmares since hearing that dangerous ominous prophecy.

"I'm sorry I woke you again." She had previously explained to Davis how she used her dreams to process her energy work with animals. It was a difficult idea for him to grasp and for most of the world, if she was entirely honest.

"You'll get uninterrupted sleep in DC." She didn't want to think about not waking in Davis' arms.

"What?"

She realized her mistake the minute the words escaped her

mouth. Her nightmare had left her feeling vulnerable, otherwise she'd never have said something so unfair. "Davis, I didn't mean it. I was trying to be funny, but it came out wrong."

"That I won't be able to comfort you is hard enough without you making jokes. God, I hate this promotion."

"I feel the same, but you're not going to the ends of the earth. And think about our weekends together."

He pressed wet kisses against her palm. "I hate that I won't be here to comfort you after a nightmare."

He followed a path along the inside of her elbow. Pleasurable streaks raced down her legs. She hadn't known her elbow could be so sensitive until Davis.

She wrapped her leg around his, rubbing herself against him. "I don't always have nightmares, only with really difficult patients like hard-headed investigators who won't believe they're in danger."

"Honey, I eventually believed you." Davis leaned on one elbow and studied her face. "But there is something else bothering you. Tell me."

Sometimes she forgot that her boyfriend was an investigator. A really good investigator. She hadn't shared her concerns about Hunter Hines. She didn't want to jeopardize Davis accepting his promotion because of the possibility of a prediction coming true.

She traced her finger along the rough stubble on his jaw. She liked his virile morning shadow, his need to shave every day. "It's been a hard few days. First, Angie and..." She almost blurted out Hunter Hines.

"Your patients don't have a clue how much you suffer with these nightmares in the course of healing them."

"They're not exactly nightmares. Most times I can let the energy move right through me, but in highly charged dreams, it's pretty diffi-cult. Dr. Z told me that he sometimes has nightmares."

"You take on their pain and heal them."

She did a disservice to Davis when she didn't think he understood. He approached her work in a logical, systematic way. He saw cause and effect, but delving into consciousness wasn't linear.

"I haven't done the actual suffering. My dreams release the tension and fears that I absorb in the treatment."

"I know a better way to release your tension. And you might want to stay awake for this incredible release, but it isn't necessary." Davis pinned her arms above her head and licked the pulse along her neck.

"You can close your eyes and sleep." He made a trail of warm kisses along the side of her breasts, her stomach. He spent a great deal of time taunting her with moist kisses around her navel and down her thighs.

Hot sensations were building. She writhed on the bed.

"Are you asleep?" her tormentor whispered in a dark, velvet voice.

He pressed her down on the bed with his heavy body and entered her in one thrust. He didn't move, but kept her arms pinned above her head. He took her breast into his mouth and suckled hard.

Pleasure and pain mixed into heady sensations. Grayce wrapped her legs around his hips and moved against him.

"Davis, please."

"Is this helping the tension?" He plunge his tongue in and out of her mouth.

"Davis," she pleaded.

"What do you want, honey?"

She tightened around him.

He let out a rush of hot air against her ear. "You shouldn't have done that." And then he began a frantic pace, taking them both over the edge.

Davis collapsed onto Grayce. He was asleep in seconds.

Grayce's eyes, however, did not close, and the waters of Lethe eluded her. Actually, nightmares were better than insomnia, she decided. She glanced over at Davis snoring with blissful satisfaction.

CHAPTER TWELVE

Grayce and James waited at the doors of University Congregational Church—wrong age, wrong clothes for the meal line for homeless youth. Even Mitzi stood out: woven collar instead of studded metal. Only Hollie, with her piercings, tattoos, and all black Goth, fit the dress code.

"Help, I'm in a nightmare. Am I at an Iggy Pop reunion?" James said sotto voce, loud enough for everyone to hear. "Please wake me up."

Unfazed, Grayce turned toward Hollie and touched her arm. "You can still change your mind. James and I can do this."

Hollie hadn't been back to Teen Feed since she started working as Grayce's receptionist. Grayce wanted to spare Hollie this glimpse of her painful, former life.

"Nah, boss. I'm good. And I wouldn't want to miss this." Hollie rolled her eyes toward James, the drama queen, with one hand on his hip.

"I can't believe you two nixed my Goth fashion statement. I would've done a lot better than this group. And I'd rock in black eyeliner," James said.

"You don't have the edge to pull it off," Hollie challenged.

"Out of the mouths of children. Me without an edge? My Grace Kelly wasn't edgy?" James and Hollie had developed the strangest and sweetest relationship. James, an only child, had adopted Hollie as his kid sister.

"They're opening the doors," Hollie said.

Their group waited as the hungry crowd filed in.

Grayce attached Mitzi's lead to the church bannister. "Sorry, girl, you have to wait outside."

Grayce swore she could hear a resigned Mitzi sigh before the poodle lay down on the sidewalk among the other dogs.

"You're not going to go around asking these kids whether they recognize Angie, are you?" James asked.

"I'm going to ask Rosemary. She's head of the program and knows all the youths. Hollie, you ask about Angie if it feels appropriate. James, just stay out of trouble."

James had wanted to come when he heard that many of the runaways were gay and escaping abusive families. Grayce had been treated to a rare moment of James' gravitas when he said, "as a community we need to do more to help these young kids. Maybe I can think of a way to help." Even Hollie had regarded him with a measure of respect.

And Davis, knowing full well that James was a fifth degree black belt, had insisted James come to protect Grayce and Hollie. She couldn't say no to Davis' over-protective demand, since he was shaken by his move to DC. She couldn't add to his stress.

James threw his head back in feigned shock. "*Moi?* Then batted his eyelashes coyly. In trouble?"

"*Oui.*" Grayce pointed at him. "Yes, you—with your critiques right out of *Project Runway* or *Top Chef*. Shall I go on?"

"Hey, Hollie." A guy about Hollie's age with at least twenty piercings on his face sauntered toward their group. He carried a battered computer with a World of Warfare logo sticker on the lid.

Hollie's face didn't show any recognition, but her body tightened imperceptibly.

"Gator," Hollie said with a snarl on her lips and in her voice. "See you're still ripping off computers."

"Oh, God. All that piercing on his gorgeous face," James said behind his hand in a theatrical whisper. "That had to hurt like a son of a bitch."

Grayce always felt at a loss when confronted with young people's self-mutilation. There had to be tremendous pain and rage for someone to destroy his face as a rebellious statement.

"I've been around," Hollie said in her tough-ass voice and widened her stance to a defensive posture. Hollie feeling threatened was never a good situation. Her assistant had never shared her experiences from her year on the street but had alluded to the violence.

"Those your parents?" Gator's lips smirked, making his assorted facial hardware undulate.

Gator was purposely baiting Hollie. She waited for James' outrageous reply but he showed incredible restraint.

Gator leaned closer to Hollie and said in a taunting tone, "Your mac daddy?"

"What the fuck?" Hollie bridged the last inches between their faces. "You sayin' I'm a ho, Gator? At least I don't hang out in the starter zones and kill all the lower level players' characters."

Hollie knew the rule of no violence at Teen Feed. Grayce didn't want this to be the moment she'd witness Hollie's progress in her Aikido training.

Grayce moved next to the combatants. "Gator, maybe you can help us. We're looking for someone, and we think she may have come here asking about her friend."

Gator looked shocked by the use of his name. Hollie kept her aggressive stance as Grayce reached into her bag. She had to dig through the lipstick, Kleenex, new CDs, acupuncture needles, and emergency bandages to reach the picture of Angie and Maddy that she had tucked into her dream/meditation journal.

Gator inspected the picture. Grayce thought she caught a glimpse of his eyes registering recognition. He shook his head. "Nah, I haven't seen them." And walked away.

"What a prick," James drew out the expletive.

"Exactly," Hollie said. "He's such a creep—gives us gamers a bad name."

"You showed amazing restraint," Grayce said to Hollie.

"You knew I wanted to flip him, didn't you, boss?"

Grayce nodded. "I did get the feeling you'd like to settle an old score."

"He's brutal, always looking to hurt someone."

"Then I'm happy that you chose not to respond to his taunts."

"It wouldn't been a fight. I'd have flipped him in one move. You would've been impressed as would've Ellen, since sometimes I don't think my mentor believes I'm making any progress."

James took the picture from Grayce. "Look at that God awful t-shirt. Who in the hell wears crap like that?"

Hollie, who had been looking over James' shoulder, said, "That's a very cool *World of Warfare* shirt."

"Both women are attractive, but like other people whose names I won't mention..." He looked at both Grayce and Hollie from their functional shoes to their ponytails. "Who don't take the time to work their assets." Only James would critique the missing women's clothing.

Last night, Grayce had searched the faces of both women for a clue, hoping to get any sense about them. She had awoken knowing that she had dreamt of them, but had no memory except frantically straining for something beyond her reach.

They walked down the stairs into the basement, a long rectangular space used for church socials and, on Tuesday nights, an outreach program for street youth.

"I wonder what they're serving. Smells like the chicken enchilada casserole," Hollie said.

"My favorite meal here," Grayce replied.

"I can't wait to try a casserole cooked in a church basement. I'm sure Teen Feed is mentioned in the Michelin Red Guide."

"What do tires have to do with a casserole?" Hollie sounded exasperated.

"Not tires. Michelin is a French review system that evaluates restaurants. If you didn't spend all your time on video games, you'd know a hell of lot more about the world."

Hollie snorted. "So I can dine out on French food?"

Grayce laughed. Hollie had definitely won this round.

In the basement, crowded with the cast-off youths, some high, others slumped in despair, Grayce was hit with the intense suffering of these kids. She took a slow, deep breath and re-focused on her goal in tonight's visit.

Hollie stopped when she saw the kids standing in line for food, as if paralyzed in an old memory.

James draped his arm around Hollie. "Come on. Let's pretend I'm your mac daddy."

Hollie rolled her dark eyes, causing her eyebrow skull-stud to bob. "There's Tom. I'll talk with him. He's one of the few normal kids. And I can do this without my mac daddy."

"I see Rosemary," Grayce said. The forty-something woman stood behind the metal counter in a white apron, matching the rest of the volunteer crew. "James, try to act inconspicuous." Had she really said that aloud? James being inconspicuous was as likely as cows flying.

Grayce turned and headed to the kitchen to find a spare apron. She planned to help out serving tonight's chicken enchilada casserole, filled with protein, and the carbs craved by the voracious youths.

The slim, animated woman beamed. "Grayce, I didn't expect you. How are you? How is Hollie?"

"Hollie's here." Grayce pointed to Hollie standing with a young man with shocking red hair streaked with blue. "I came to ask you about a patient of mine."

"Another troublesome cat?" Rosemary was a cat lover who loved to joke about Grayce's challenging patients.

Rosemary also teased Grayce that her compassion was wasted on silly, pampered cats. Grayce understood the teen's hurt, it reminded her of her own painful adolescence after her sister's death.

"My patient is a wonderful cat. Her owner, Angie, is missing."

"I'm sorry." Rosemary knew full well what "missing" meant to a young woman.

"Angie's friend might have been a regular here. Could you look at her picture?"

"Of course."

Grayce handed the picture to Rosemary who scrutinized each face. Grayce wondered how many times Barbara had been asked to identify a missing kid.

"I know Maddy," Rosemary said.

"You do?" Hope surged through Grayce.

"She was a regular here until she joined the Marines. Best thing that ever happened for her. When she came back here a few weeks ago and looked like she was using again, it hit me hard. You get so excited when any kid gets off the street and finds a life."

Grayce touched Rosemary's arm and spoke softly. "Your job is tough here on the front line. Don't give up on Maddy. She has a friend who really cares for her."

Grayce pointed out Angie in the picture. "This is the woman. Angie went missing after she announced that she intended to bring Maddy back from the streets. I'm helping Angie's mom."

"You aren't the first to ask about Maddy. A guy showed me a picture of the same woman. Said Angie was his stepsister."

"Stepsister?" That Angie wasn't Hunter's sister may have explained his lack of concern, but it didn't explain his lack of compassion for Mrs. Hines.

"I didn't tell him anything. I don't give information about clients to anyone, especially to people saying they're family." Rosemary's voice vibrated with intensity. "Our kids' families can be dangerous to their lives."

Rosemary, who had never been protected in her life, fiercely guarded the safety of her charges.

"I've met the brother. I don't believe he wishes his sister any harm." Grayce felt certain that Hunter wouldn't hurt Angie, but she was still struggling with his suspicious behavior and Aunt Aideen's prediction.

"Doesn't matter. I don't give out information. I tell the youths when someone is looking for them, then they can decide if they want to see them."

Grayce suspected that Hollie had to hide from her father for her own safety. Grayce would never ask. From her work with abused animals, Grayce had learned that trust was a slow and fragile balance.

"Did Angie come here looking for Maddy?" Grayce was breathless; if so, this might be a real lead.

"Yes, she did. Angie explained that she and Maddy had been in Afghanistan together. And that they were in PTSD group together when Maddy disappeared. I could tell she wanted to help Maddy."

"Did you know where Maddy was crashing or who she was hanging with?"

"No. And Maddy hasn't been here since Angie came looking for her, as if she didn't want to be found. Angie was frustrated by my lack of information."

Grayce tried not to show her disappointment. "Was there anything else that Angie asked?"

"I did tell her that Maddy came in twice with a guy that I had never seen before. Not one of our regulars."

"Her drug dealer?" Grayce asked.

"Never know for sure, but he didn't seem familiar with any of our users. He didn't approach anyone. Kept to himself."

"What did he look like?"

"Tall, dark."

"Anything else?"

If Rosemary said, "handsome", then Grayce decided she would start to question her own sanity.

"Anything else?"

"He kept scanning the room as if he was looking for someone."

"Maybe a dealer hoping to score a sale?"

"I don't know why, but I don't think so. Maybe it was his beard."

"He had a beard?" Grayce shuddered as her premonition floated up.

"Never seen anything like it—narrow and went down to his chest. What a bizarre statement. And I'm more than used to bizarre with our kids' piercings and tattoos.

"Can you describe anything else about this guy? I'm not sure if there's any connection, but anything leading to Maddy might help us find Angie."

"He kept his hoodie up so I didn't see his hair. But I remembered he had sunglasses on, so I never saw his eyes."

"Would you call me if Maddy or that guy comes in? I'd like to ask them about Angie."

"Sure. I'd love to help you could find Maddy and her friend."

"Do you need help serving or cleaning up?"

The youths started to get into the food line. Hollie was still in conversation with her friend Tom. Her body was relaxed, and she was smiling.

"Thanks for the offer. I've got tonight covered."

"I'm sorry that I'm not one of your volunteers any longer, but my practice keeps me pretty busy." She didn't add "and my boyfriend."

"You and your parents have done so much for Teen Feed."

Grayce's parents had made a sizable donation in her sister Cassie's memory.

"Taking care of the kids' pets when no one else will is really great. You know what their animals mean to them after their families' rejections."

"I love helping."

"You did a wonderful thing by hiring Hollie," Rosemary said. "Look at her now. She was such an angry woman, and rightfully so."

Both women turned to look at a laughing Hollie as she punched her friend in the arm.

"Hollie has become an essential part of my practice. Can't imagine the office without her," Grayce said. "Thanks, Rosemary. We'll be heading out."

Grayce looked for James who sat at a table with a withdrawn kid in thick glasses and terrible acne. Whatever James had said cracked the kid up.

Grayce caught James' eye and signaled to meet at the door. James shook hands with the young man and walked over to meet Grayce.

She'd like to acknowledge James' touching connection to the obviously lonely kid, but James didn't like any attention to his good deeds.

"I'm impressed with what they do here for these kids," James said.

"They're always looking for volunteers."

James looked quite serious. "Once I get off the housing board, I might start volunteering here. Of course, just to give these kids some fashion tips."

There was her familiar cynical friend.

James and Grayce waited at the bottom of the steps for Hollie.

Hollie hugged her friend Tom and walked toward them. "Boss. Tom knows where Maddy has been crashing."

Grayce rubbed her arm with the sudden chill. "What?"

"He crashed there a couple of times, but said the guy Maddy is hanging with is really weird."

"This is great news."

"Nice work, kid," James said. "And I can't wait to go to this fashionable location."

Grayce elbowed James in the stomach.

"Where is it?" Grayce asked.

"The condemned house on 65th. It's all boarded up, but I'm sure I can figure out how to get in."

"Exactly my kind of Tuesday night—breaking into condemned buildings," James quipped in his sardonic tone.

"James, you could stay here and clean up." Hollie raised one pierced eyebrow in question.

"That's a great idea. We'll pick you up after we're done investigating," Grayce added.

"Very funny, ladies. You know you need me for my fighting skills."

"Honey, we don't need you." Hollie emphasized the "honey" the same way James did. "The boss and I both do Aikido."

"Let's face it, 'the boss' really doesn't like doing Aikido, and you're a fledgling." James laughed.

James was right. Grayce had learned Aikido as a way of learning how to control and focus energy for her healing work, not for martial arts combat. She might need to start practicing Aikido since her dreams had become darker and filled with gloomy, hateful energy.

"You need me. I'm a manly deterrent."

Hollie snorted. "Manly? You wore all black to fit in, but your clothes scream money and fashion."

"That's the nicest thing you've said to me. And my personal shopper at Mario's is going to be very happy to have received your seal of fashion approval."

Hollie sniggered.

CHAPTER THIRTEEN

James got into the front seat of Grayce's Subaru with Hollie and Mitzi in the back.

Mitzi sat alert, looking out the window as if she knew they were on a mission. Grayce drove north ten blocks to a row of condemned houses from the early 20th Century that had long since given up their families to students, squatters and squirrels, and now awaited the inevitable bulldozers that would convert them into public transportation. Although 8:30 at night, the sun was shining. The days were long in Seattle's summer, making up for the short, dark days of November.

"I hope the house hasn't been knocked down with the new light rail going in," James said.

"Nah, Tom said he stayed there two weeks ago."

"The way Seattle is destroying buildings, I wouldn't be so sure," James added.

Grayce parked the car on the street at the intersection of 65th and 15th. "We're here."

Climbing out of the car, they had a good view of the old house with the yellow condemned tape.

"This house has good bones. It's too bad the owner didn't take care of her. She could still be a beauty. Makes me sad to see turn of the century houses left in disrepair."

Grayce always appreciated James' love of visual aesthetics. Grayce missed a lot of the visual because of her absorption with the unseen world of energy. "Let's just scope it out and walk around the building. I'm not up for breaking in," Grayce said.

"Look at the garbage," James said as they went around to the back of the house. The backyard was covered in discarded fast food containers and plastic bags. "There are going to be rats in there." James visibly shuddered.

Apprehension skidded down Grayce's spine as if someone were watching her. She turned around a full 360 degrees and didn't see anyone, but she couldn't stop her heart from racing.

The back door was partially opened. "I've stayed in places a lot worse than this," Hollie said without any emotion.

Grayce's stomach knotted with the reminder of Hollie's past life. Grayce had volunteered at Teen Feed, but she had never really known the dreadful reality of what it meant to live on the streets.

James didn't make his usual irreverent joke, but remained silent as if he also had taken in the horror of Hollie's past.

"I'll go in." The familiar, tough-ass Hollie was back. "I'm not intimidated by rats."

"You don't have to go in. We can yell from the door," Grayce said.

"If there is anyone in there who doesn't want to be disturbed, it could be dangerous. People take offense when someone invades their territory," Hollie said.

"I'll go with Mitzi. I wore my Lanvin lace-up trainers just for this moment. Remember, I'm the professional here." James walked toward the uneven steps.

"Professional? A professional fashionista?" Hollie skirted ahead of James.

"Professional architect. But I'm going to come out crying when I see the destruction of this house. Rather like an aging Greta Garbo."

Hollie rolled her eyes.

Grayce couldn't stop the feeling of uneasiness—a tingling on the back of her neck, as if someone were behind her. She turned around. There was nothing there but the scattered litter.

"I'll go first." James climbed the first two rotting steps and looked down on Grayce and Hollie. "Wait here."

"I'll go. I'm the experienced squatter." Hollie took the steps and stood on the back porch.

James laughed out loud. "Experienced squatter. I'm not going to say a word. My lips are zipped." He made the zipper motion, right out of first grade.

While the two stood arguing, Grayce with Mitzi walked around them and through the back door. Mitzi's body had tensed. "Hello, anyone here?"

No answer except the scurrying of small paws.

"Oh, my God. The smell...this horrific smell might kill me." James stood behind Grayce. "Why did I wear my new Ermenegildo Zegna pants? I'll never get the smell out."

Hollie, who followed behind, was prepared to plunge through the debris in her black combat boots. The boots weren't just a rebellious fashion statement but practical for squatting.

James and Grayce, with their flashlight apps to light the way, entered the dining room. Like the kitchen, there were blocks of concrete spread throughout the grimy room, possibly used for shelves by poor students once upon a time.

Garbage bags, some with refuse, some with belongings, were scattered willy-nilly through the space. Old mattresses were thrown on the living room floor with half-burned candles. A shopping cart sat in the far corner brimming with more of the black garbage bags.

"I'll check out the upstairs." The sound of the creaking wood echoed in the space as Hollie ascended the rutted wood steps. She yelled down. "No one here but definitely people have been crashing here. Looks like they cleared out."

Grayce didn't question how Hollie could tell that the residents had left the house.

Although the house was uninhabited, Grayce felt the human misery in this empty, depressing space. What hope could you have without a safe, clean place to live?

"I need to go home and shower in gallons of hot water. I don't know if I'm ever going to feel clean again," James whined.

"Hush. Hollie used to live in places like this," Grayce whispered.

"Boss, I'm cool." Hollie stood on the last step.

"Well, thank the Lord she doesn't live here now." James' voice was fierce with suppressed emotion.

Mitzi strained on her lead, pulling toward one of the concrete blocks in the center of the dining room. She sniffed at the dark spot on the floor. "What is it, Mitzi?"

Grayce pointed to the reddish brown spot. "Do you think that's blood on the floor?" A harsh disquiet settled in her.

The dog continued to sniff around the concrete block.

"Might be, but I don't want to imagine other body fluids. Let's get the 'f' out of here."

They walked single file out through the kitchen. James led, Grayce and Mitzi followed in the middle, Hollie brought up the rear.

They all breathed deeply the fresh air as they emerged outside. Although the backyard was littered, a breeze brought much-needed relief. The sun was starting to fade into the west.

Grayce leaned over the railing on the back porch, searching the yard and the area beneath the porch. She couldn't shake her anxiety of another presence.

"What is it, Grayce? You got the heebie-jeebies too?"

"Guess so." Grayce didn't want to discuss the dark suffering in the house or her concern that someone was watching them. "I'm with James, let's get out of here."

Grayce realized that the intensity of the malevolence focused on her was immense; that it was far out of proportion to anything rational. It was insane. Fear sped up her heart—but she wouldn't tell the others. They would want to investigate, and this was like kids playing with blasting caps. This wasn't some belligerent squatter that James or Hollie could put in a headlock if necessary—this was someone full of deadly, cold rage. She had to get them out of here. At her side Mitzi growled. Grayce tightened her hand on the leash. "No Mitzi. No chasing squirrels today. Come on."

They all proceeded out through the gate in the metal fence surrounding the property.

"Are you going to call Mrs. Hines tonight?" Hollie asked.

"I'll call her tomorrow. There isn't anything she can do tonight. Hunter already knows that Angie went to Teen Feed. I'm sure Angie came to the house to look for Maddy, but there isn't any proof." Grayce was disappointed that she didn't have more to offer Mrs. Hines. But at least this was a beginning.

"She can call the police and have them come out here and look around. Might be something in the rubble," Grayce said.

"If that was blood on the floor," Hollie said, "maybe they could do a DNA sample?"

"You've been watching too much CSI. No way they can get DNA from that spot," James said.

"You don't know," Hollie challenged.

"You're right. I don't." James laughed. "T-squares and protractors for me—not test tubes and body fluids."

They walked around the house to 65th street.

"Not sure what it means. Did Angie find Maddy? Go with her? But why would they both disappear? Doesn't make sense. And why haven't the police found Angie or Maddy?" Grayce spoke the questions out loud, as if hearing her own thoughts might reveal some logic.

"I'll never be able to wear these shoes again." James looked down at his beige, canvas shoes.

"If Maddy wants to hide from the police, she can easily stay under the radar," Hollie said.

"What do you mean stay under the radar?" Grayce asked as she dug into the side pocket of her purse for her keys.

Hollie opened the back door for Mitzi to jump in.

"If you're on the run, you evade detection by changing locations."

Grayce's stomach clenched with the knowledge that Hollie knew too much about being on the run. What had this young woman lived through?

"You don't stay in the same spot. I'm not trying to be a bummer, but the chance that Maddy left anything for the police to find is small. Sounds like she's lived on the streets before."

"But we do know that Maddy is hanging with that weird guy with the beard. That might give the police a lead if Tom describes him," Grayce said.

"Tom won't talk to the police. You'll have to do it."

"I'll give Mrs. Hines the information, and if the police want to talk with me, that's fine."

"I'm not sure, Grayce, that it's a good idea for you to share that we broke into the house," James said.

"I'll tell Mrs. Hines about going to the house but let the police search the house again."

Grayce had no clear vision about Angie's presence, but she somehow knew the woman wasn't dead.

CHAPTER FOURTEEN

Brandon stood behind the Cypress tree and watched three people and a French Poodle go into the house. What the fuck was with the poodle? He immediately recognized the take-charge attitude in the pert, blonde woman. She had the same determined look as his mother.

Watching the smiling woman brought all the horrendous feelings back. His mother, pushing, pushing, always pushing. His gut twisted into a tight knot. His hands fisted at his sides.

He'd moved his shit from the house after Gator told him a dude who looked like a cop was asking questions about Maddy and his missing sister. He had Gator stationed at Teen Feed, watching for anyone asking questions.

No one gave a shit about Maddy, but her friend obviously had people looking for her. He didn't tell Maddy about the search.

Maddy didn't give a rat's ass about her military friend or oil tankers threatening the Orcas in Harrow Straight. She mouthed the ecoterrorists platitudes. He recognized in Maddy the same insatiable rage to destroy.

He strained forward, attempting to hear the intruders. The

blonde turned around as if she sensed him lurking in the trees. Stupid-ass yuppies clustered together on the back porch to discuss whether to trespass. It'd be hilarious if they weren't playing a dangerous game.

The woman with the ink had been around, but the other two in their expensive threads definitely belonged with his parents at the tennis club on Mercer Island.

Like his decisive, surgeon-mother, the blonde woman led the group into the house. They wouldn't find anything. He had moved the materials to Pioneer Square and planned to keep moving the stuff until D-day.

He waited in the trees. A damn poodle wasn't trained to detect explosives, but he had to make sure. He was getting paranoid.

The woman led the group out of the house after only ten minutes. The guy had the most hilarious look of disgust on his face. Bet he never got a smell like that in his penthouse.

He leaned in further, enjoying the little game of cat-and-mouse with the bitch. She scanned the yard again as if she suspected his presence in the trees. The dude definitely wanted to get away.

They faced away from him as they went down the steps, but he clearly heard the bitch say that she was going to call the police. What the fuck?

Another memory raced into his brain—his mother, with tears in her eyes, telling him she had to tell his father about his latest lapse with the law, but she'd soften his father's rage.

He had been shipped off to military school so his father wouldn't be reminded of his one failure—his son. His mother thought it was for the best.

The bitch was doing all the talking, but he couldn't hear. He'd need to follow them to find out about her and her meddling.

CHAPTER FIFTEEN

G rayce sat alone in her office—rare that Hollie and Mitzi, who spent most days at Grayce's office, would both be absent. Hollie had gone for Grayce's favorite lunch, a Vietnamese veggie Banh mi. Grayce had sent Mitzi to Davis' office, anticipating that her next patient, a military bomb-sniffing dog, needed a non-threatening space.

The click of canine nails on the wood floor announced the arrival of her client. She restacked her charts and walked to the office door.

Talley and the sergeant stood in the doorway. Not surprising, the Golden Lab was on high alert. Her lean, muscular body was tense. With the leash gripped tightly in his broad hand, the man and dog both looked combat-ready.

"I'm Grayce Walters. You must be Sergeant Welby and Talley." Talley's ears flicked at the mention of her name.

"Yes, ma'am." Despite his close-cropped hair and military posture, the blond sergeant had a boyish vitality reflecting his youth.

"Please, come into my office. My receptionist is on an errand."

Talley walked next to her handler, eyes focused ahead. Her nose twitched, searching for a scent. Talley was fully engaged, on the lookout for danger.

"Please have a seat." Grayce indicated the chair across from her desk.

The sergeant sat with his spine erect and not touching the back of the chair.

Grayce sat down behind her desk. "Talley is a beautiful dog."

Grayce didn't mention highly strung-out. The anxiety radiating from the dog and handler was palpable.

"Thank you, ma'am. She is one of the best we have. She is relentless when she's on a mission. She can work for hours."

Both man and dog were locked in, ready to spring into action. They had good reason to be vigilant. The sergeant had been injured in an IED explosion in Afghanistan. Their world had proven to be unpredictable and dangerous.

"I'm a bit surprised by Talley's breed. I thought the military used Belgian Malinois, Dutch and German Shepherds. Golden Labs are more likely to be companion dogs, since they aren't known for their aggression."

"Talley is one of the few Golden Labs in the military. Her Labrador nose combined with her Golden Retriever focus and loyalty make her a perfect soldier."

"I can see her incredible concentration, but away from the battlefield she might have trouble turning her intense focus off."

"Yes, ma'am. It's been hard for both of us to adjust." The sergeant's eyes were war-weary and drained.

Both dog and man's haunted look attested that they had suffered and were still suffering. Her job was to help them feel safe again.

"I see that Mike Samson referred you. I'm surprised. I thought his veterinary practice was horses."

"Yes, ma'am, he treats only horses. My family raises horses in Auburn. Doc Samson has been our family vet since Doc Corin retired. You came down to Auburn and treated one of Doc Samson's patients. He thought you might be able to help Talley."

"I did treat one of Mike's racehorses." Grayce chuckled. "You should've seen Mike's face when I arrived. I wasn't the vet he was expecting." She was consciously trying to ease the strain in the room. She gestured, reaching toward the ceiling. "Probably a much bigger woman."

The sergeant laughed. With his enjoyment, the muscles above Talley's eyes relaxed.

"The horse was seventeen hands and nervous. I was able to calm him and treat his injured knee."

"Doc Samson said he wouldn't have believed what you did if he hadn't seen for himself. He was really impressed, which is saying a lot. Doc Samson is a man of few words."

"I was able to help the horse, and I'll be able to help Talley." She wanted the sergeant to know she wasn't afraid of their demons.

"I've read the referral from Mike," she said, wanting to protect Talley from hearing her symptoms recounted. Discussing anxiety heightened fears. "Is Talley still taking the Prozac that the military veterinarian prescribed?"

"No, ma'am. I weaned her off of it. I just couldn't drug her anymore. Didn't seem right. We've both been working out and running more to get rid of the jitters."

"Will Talley allow me to approach her with you sitting here?" Grayce already knew she could approach Talley but wanted to respect her handler.

"No problem, ma'am. She isn't aggressive. She's very protective of me, and I do worry some when people approach me. She's been through a lot."

"I'm not surprised that Talley would be more protective after your injury."

"Since the explosion, she's become hyper-vigilant and listless. It's the reason she's on military leave. The vet doesn't know if she'll ever have her determination to work again."

"I don't have a lot of experience working with military dogs, but I've treated loads of anxious animals. Right now, Talley's using lots of energy to suppress the anticipation that something terrible is going to happen. Once I help her release the fear, she'll get her energy back."

Grace stood. "She's a young dog?"

"Five years old."

Grayce walked around her desk and spoke in her quiet, gentle voice. "She's got lots of years of working and playing ahead of her."

Talley remained on alert. Her soft, tired eyes focused on Grayce. The dog had remained calm, non-aggressive—her muscles hadn't tensed, and her fur hadn't bristled in warning.

Grayce, in her usual blue jeans, slowly knelt down next to the dog. "You can relax, Talley. This office is a safe place."

Grayce looked up at the sergeant. "Let's have Talley lie down."

"Yes, ma'am." The sergeant gave one tug on Talley's lead. "Talley, down."

Talley lay on her stomach but her spine was rigid, still ready to jump into battle.

Grayce had taken the precaution to bring the acupuncture needles in her pocket. It was best to minimize the activity in the room.

"You're doing a great job protecting Sergeant Welby. He isn't in any danger now. He's safe, and so are you, Talley." Grayce moved her hands above the yellow dog's back to assess heat.

Talley stretched out her front paws—her first non-threatening movement since she had arrived.

"You are a solider, Talley." Grayce used a relaxed tone, a humming mantra. "And sometimes soldiers need to rest." With her hands still above the dog, Grayce closed her eyes and tried to shift the frenetic energy swirling around Talley.

Bright, hot lights burst beneath Grayce's eyelids. She absorbed the burning heat of the volatile energy stored in Talley's body. Visualizing a rushing waterfall, the sound of cool water flowing over smooth rocks, Grayce envisioned the frenetic fear leaving Talley's body, moving down the sun-dappled stream.

She threaded the tiny needles along both sides of Talley's vertebrae to open the flow of stagnant chi. She focused on regulating the liver by placing needles at the Curved Spring, the center of stored emotions, on the inside of each back leg.

As Grayce rotated the liver points, Talley laid her head on her front paws and slept. She whispered close to Talley's ear. "You got the job done with your fierce heart. You can rest now." Grayce balanced the needles on Talley's head and spine one last time. "You protected Sergeant Welby and brought him home, like the good solider you are. It's time to let go of the fear."

Grayce pretended not to notice the tears gathering in the sergeant's eyes. Her deep place always brought the words to heal.

After Grayce removed the needles, Talley rolled to her side and slept against the sergeant's leg.

Grayce walked to the cabinet. She busied herself for a few minutes to give the sergeant time to compose himself.

"Thank you, ma'am, for what you just did. I haven't seen Talley relax since the day we got injured."

"You're welcome. Acupuncture will help Talley calm down. Have you ever drunk too much caffeine, sergeant? To the point that your heart's speeding, your perceptions are super-acute, your skin hurts because you're revved up?"

"Yes, ma'am. That's every day in Afghanistan. You're always wound up because you and your unit's existence depends on remaining focused."

Talley and Sergeant Welby had survived four years in Afghanistan by remaining vigilant—not an easy transition coming home. "I'd like to treat Talley once a week for the next three months. Auburn is not close. Will it be a problem? "

"Not a problem, ma'am. I'd do anything for this dog."

"Do you swim, sergeant?"

His eyes widened in question. "Excuse me?"

"I'd like you and Talley to start swimming in a lake or deep river. It's important that you do it together."

"I do swim, ma'am, and Lake Youngs is close by our family farm."

"Water will soothe Talley's ratcheted up nervous system." Grayce omitted. "And yours, too."

They both needed to float, to suspend the pressure on their nervous systems. Getting them into the water would be a beginning.

"Don't do any training around the swimming. Talley needs a real break from her work. Her senses, especially her focus and her nose, are working overtime. She'll have a break in the water."

Grayce used water therapy for injuries and arthritis, but had never before prescribed hydrotherapy for anxiety.

"Let's see how this week goes. I can hear that my assistant is back. She'll make your appointment for next week."

———

Hollie stood on a stool and reached into the cupboard above the file cabinet. With her back to the door, she was unaware of an audience. Grayce was afraid to speak and startle Hollie.

The sergeant's entire body tightened at the sight of Hollie in her short skirt. She heard him take a deep breath.

Hollie hummed a Nirvana song as she searched in the back of the cupboard. Her tight skirt rode higher giving a full view of her upper thighs in fishnet stockings.

Under his breath, Sergeant Welby said something in a desperate tone. Grayce was pretty sure she heard. "Oh, hell."

Hollie turned quickly with the sound and almost fell backward into the cabinet.

"I didn't hear you come out of the office." Hollie jumped off the stool in one agile move unfazed by her high-heeled boots.

Hollie and the sergeant locked eyes for several seconds, neither uttering a sound. Grayce watched, fascinated. She could almost see the sparks flowing between them.

"Galachel!" The sergeant broke the awkward silence. His eyes were focused on Hollie's black t-shirt with a mythical female figure with flowing golden hair. Unlike last week's avenging goddess, this woman was ephemeral and mystical.

Her chatty office assistant was dumbstruck. A wash of color crossed her cheeks. "You know...Galachel?" Her voice came out in a breathless whisper.

The sergeant angled his body closer to Hollie. "The radiant daughter."

The charge between the two people was electrifying. Grayce hated to interrupt the painfully wonderful moment.

"Hollie, can you give Talley and Sergeant Welby..."

"Please call me Nick." His lowered voice was focused toward Hollie.

Hollie looked young and sweet despite her heavy metal piercings and tattoos. Grayce sometimes forgot Hollie's young age.

"Can you make an appointment for Nick and Talley next week?" Grayce asked.

"Can do." Hollie bent over Talley and rubbed her head. "What an amazing dog."

Talley, relaxed from the acupuncture treatment and sensing Hollie's empathy, raised her head to continue the petting.

Nick eased his tight control on Talley's lead. His face had softened, and his lips parted in a smile.

Hollie looked up into Nick's face and whatever she saw caused the red to creep up her neck and face.

Grayce remembered the first moment she had looked into Davis' eyes, and she felt an amazingly joyful and exhilarating connection.

Grayce cleared her throat. "I'll look forward to seeing you next week."

Grayce hummed "Smells Like Teen Spirit" as she walked into her office. Moments like this were important to savor. The universe had provided a serendipitous path to help heal the sergeant.

CHAPTER SIXTEEN

The dappled sunlight shone on Dr. Z's round, brown face, creating the beatific countenance of an enlightened saint. The ritual was always the same; Grayce smiled then her mentor smiled.

His stillness washed over her, opening her to his deep gaze. In the brief moment's exchange, she couldn't hide from his soul scrutiny.

"How are you?" As part of the ritual, he always asked, but he already knew.

There was deep serenity in the garden, as if he poured his peaceful energy into each plant, as he did when he prepared each cup of hot tea for her.

Unlike his modest demeanor, his garden was a messy abandon of riotous blossoming foxglove, sweet peas, and bright colored roses surrounding the statue of a bodhisattva, a compassionate saint who stays on earth to alleviate suffering. As in everything Dr. Z touched, his loving care radiated, enveloping her in stillness.

She wrapped her hands around the cup and drifted into the calmness.

Dr. Z waited. He always waited. He never rushed.

She had organized her thoughts on the drive to the Ravenna neighborhood, expecting to discuss them with Dr. Z, but as often occurred, the concerns floated away.

Then abruptly she blurted out, "I'm having terrible nightmares."

His head tilted toward her. He listened with his whole body and heart.

"Each night I'm either reliving the moment my sister died or I'm being burned alive. The dreams vary but not the feelings. There is always...deep pain and deep fear."

Grayce was sinking into the familiar black emptiness of loss. Dr. Z elicited her innermost feelings.

His calm voice pulled her back. "You're still trying to find the missing soldier, yes?"

Grayce was puzzled—but then she realized he was talking about Angie. "I am."

"The mother is grieving, like your mother did when you were a young girl?"

A dull ache started behind her eyes.

"Your lesson was so very big for someone so very small." He absorbed her pain. "The shock of abandonment, very hard at such an early age."

The tears welled up in her eyes, and it surprised her that she could still tap into the raw, intense pain, as though it had been yesterday—instead of decades ago. She let Dr. Z's words wash over and envelop her.

"A blessing to learn this lesson." Dr. Z had tried to bring her along the path to realize essential solitude was important to finding the stillness and the blessedness in yourself. "The pain in your life gives you a wonderful patina, like my teapot." He lifted the pot, turning the 19th century vessel that he used in all of their sessions.

"Did you know that I pour hot tea over the pot each day to prevent the clay from drying out? The hot tea gives the pot its beautiful patina. If I didn't follow the ritual, the pot would crumble."

"I'm not surprised that Mrs. Hines' grief brings up my grief, but why am I back in this dark place? I've healed myself and moved forward. Why is the pain as acute as when Cassie died?"

He leaned over and touched her hand. The connection was intense. "But you're not living in the pain as you did when you were a little girl. It's only in your dreams."

Dr. Z's words were balm to her soul. "You're peeling away another layer of your loss with these dreams."

"I've tried to protect myself against feeling the pain again."

"But something else has triggered this feeling of loss? Yes? Not just the grieving mother."

There was no fooling her mentor.

"Davis is moving to Washington DC for at least six months, possibly a year."

Dr. Z's dark eyes were filled with compassion. He sifted through all the words and delved deep into her heart. "You love this man, yes?"

She nodded. There was no stopping the tears from pouring out.

"There is much fear, deep in your heart." He patted his heart. "But your dreams are healing you, making you ready to let go of the fear and love this man."

His healing words smoothed the jagged edges of her pain, the sleepless nights.

"Tell me about the fires in your dreams."

"The missing woman—soldier survived IED bomb explosions in Afghanistan. Recently, I started treating a military dog and her master who both experienced similar explosions. I've assumed I had absorbed their fear and pain around fire."

"It's a heavy load to take on a client's pain, but you must feel the pain in order to heal."

The sweet acknowledgment hung in the air like the lyrical garden chimes. Like a magical alchemist, he changed her pain into light and love, enabling her to treat others.

"That is why you come here, yes?" Another joyous smile. The colors in the garden grew brighter.

"There is more to the fire dreams than your client's pain."

"Yes, I feel it, too. My tarot card reading by Davis' aunt warned me of danger from a tall, dark man."

"Spiritual paths may take many names and forms." Dr. Z nodded. "You believe this prediction?"

"Aunt Aideen immediately recognized my talents. And I don't believe she'd have shared the prediction if she didn't believe in the danger."

"Yes, I can feel the danger also."

"I thought the missing woman's brother was possibly the threat, but now I'm not sure."

Dr. Z leaned forward in his chair.

"I didn't tell Davis about the prediction."

"You didn't want him to be upset with his aunt." His lips revealed a hint of a smile.

"Yes."

It was always the same. Dr. Z understood and simplified her worries into acceptance.

"And you're protecting the aunt and Davis. Yes? And you know that his aunt has gifts that he doesn't understand."

She was always amazed by her mentor's ability to look right into her heart. She thought of herself as a gifted intuitive, but in comparison to Dr. Z, she was a neophyte.

Dr. Z chuckled. The delightful sound pealed in the garden like the birdsong on the wind, jubilant music that your heart hears.

"I will treat you today. Acupuncture will help you with the fear and pain."

CHAPTER SEVENTEEN

It had been a long and difficult day. Davis was relieved to be seated at la Spiga with a glass of deep ruby Valpolicella in his hand and Grayce's radiant face across the table. She reached over and gently touched his hand. Grayce always knew when he was stressed.

"How was your first meeting with the Fusion Center folks?" She ran her hand over his and looked deeply into his eyes. It was strange how she did that, but he felt calmer.

"Way too much to learn about the different agencies and how they collaborate for a single mission. Actually, it was rather refreshing to have a clear focus."

"Clear focus?"

"Arson investigations are pretty messy and unsatisfying. There is a very low success rate of nailing the bastards."

"I looked up the Fusion Center's website and couldn't help glancing at some of the conspiracy websites about it, too. They make it sound like a sexy thriller with all the involved agencies— Like a Bourne movie filled with danger and intrigue."

"Sexy?" His voice got husky. She had that playful gleam in her eye that always ignited his primitive responses. Grayce definitely knew how to lighten every inch of his foul mood.

"Sexy is you in those sandals with the ribbons...and nothing else."

"What?" Grayce's eyes widened.

He loved her shocked but sensual look. "I loved our night after the Mariners game."

"You've thought of me in the espadrilles and nothing else?"

"Honey, I think about you 'in nothing else' all the time."

He was only teasing her, but he was going to be in trouble soon. It wasn't helping that Grayce was rubbing his hand in just the way he liked her to rub him.

He took a deep breath. "What did you ask me?"

Grayce laughed. The light, joyful sound soothed the ragged edges of his mind from the overwhelming details of his new position.

"I asked you about your Fusion meeting and whether it felt like a thriller movie."

"Only in that there was a room filled with a team of tech experts in front of computer screens feeding Bourne the information. Today we got briefed by Homeland Security on the present threat analysis in the Pacific Northwest."

"Our threat level is pretty high because of our nuclear submarine bases and our Canadian border, right? Can you tell me what was said or is it classified?"

"The presentation wasn't anything specific, but the most interesting part was the expectation of increased threats from Eco-terrorists."

"Eco-terrorists?"

"With the increase in oil tankers in the Puget Sound, the environmental risks to the marine life increase. Canadian oil tankers are coming through Harrow Straight, the breeding waters for the Orca whales."

The playful spark disappeared in Grayce's eyes.

"What is it, Grayce?"

"The idea of an oil tanker spilling in our beautiful water is horrible...unimaginable."

Damn it. Why in hell was he upsetting Grayce? She took in the world in such a different way, absorbing the life force. It was a hard balance for him between wanting to share and, at the same time, protect. He definitely wouldn't bring up the oil trains coming through Seattle.

"Let's order. Should we get our usual?" he asked.

Grayce always had the shrimp diablo, and he had the lasagna. He liked the idea that they had a "usual." They were building a lot of "usuals" together when he was about to leave. He had decided to avoid all mention of his leaving since it was ruining their time together. They had six weeks before he left, and he wasn't going to emphasize the most difficult part.

"Did you remember to ask your sister what I should bring to the party?"

"No, damn it. I forgot. I'll text her right now." He poured Grayce more wine and then texted his sister.

Grayce sipped her wine.

"My sisters are very excited to meet you. They've been bugging me for weeks to bring you over. If it weren't a family tradition to do the Fourth of July party, I'd swear they were throwing it just to meet you."

"Did your sisters like Daphne?"

Grayce surprised him. She had never asked before about his relationship with Daphne.

"They never said anything about Daphne until we broke up, and then they couldn't stop talking about how much they didn't like her. He could imagine his sisters' reaction if they ever found out about Daphne and Rod.

"I'm sure they're very protective of you. You're their special big brother."

"I might be special, but they sure both love to boss me around."

Grayce looked at him tenderly, as if she understood how much his sisters meant to him.

"Were your parents upset that you wouldn't be going out to Hood Canal with them?" he asked.

"No, they understood."

"It's too bad they're going out of town, or we could've invited them to the party.'

Grayce looked up from the menu. "I hadn't thought about it."

She hadn't thought about it. That stung. For the last three months, he had tiptoed around the fact that Grayce hadn't introduced him to her parents yet. He had wanted her to meet his sisters, but had waited because of Grayce's hesitation about commitment.

"I've been looking at the weeks in the fall and wanted to see if you looked at your schedule so we could plan your visit to DC. I'll be totally settled by early September and you could come out. Maybe block out all your appointments for that week"

"I know it's hard to leave the Northwest in September, but the fall on the East Coast is beautiful. Maybe we could drive up the coast or go to New York City. That's the great thing about the East Coast— everything is close."

Grayce's usual shining eyes were dimmed and hard to read. He had decided not to talk about the future, but instead he brought up the fall. What was he doing?

"You are going to come out to DC, right?"

"I will. I'm not sure when yet. Do you really need to know now? Tonight?"

He could feel the tension mounting in his body. "I don't need a date, but I need to know that you're planning to come."

"Of course I will."

And he could feel her inner sigh of impatience with him. "Tell me."

"You're more stressed since you've taken the new job. And I feel the pressure."

"What is that supposed to mean?"

"You want to control how our relationship should happen, put us on a timetable. I thought we agreed to enjoy the time and not pressure the each other."

"I know, but my leaving changes all of that."

"How does it change things?" Her eyes were focused on his face, searching.

He felt as if he were stepping into the abyss. "How are we going to keep our relationship growing if we don't plan to see each other?"

"We are going to see each other, but we don't need a spreadsheet to plan it all out."

Maybe she understood him better than he thought.

"We agreed not to pressure each other over a long term commitment. Our plan was to spend time together." She shook her head. "I don't know how to do this...us."

His heart thudded against his chest.

Grayce's blond hair hung down around her face and hid her from his inspection. He needed to see her eyes to understand.

"Life changes without warning. One minute everything is wonderful, and the next everything comes crashing down." There was something bleak and awful in her voice.

"But you can't curtail your life because bad might happen. Honey, making plans isn't such a big deal."

"You don't understand. You thrive on danger. Your job is unsafe, and you climb mountains for fun." Her face turned pale, making her green eyes shine brighter.

He wasn't sure that he followed Grayce's convoluted thinking, but his gut knew where this was leading. She was putting up barriers.

"I don't want to stop you from doing what you love, but you live your life as if death isn't a possibility. I know it is. I worry that if I commit, I'll be living the rest of my life in fear of losing you."

He felt as if he had been sucker-punched. If he said anything at this point, he'd sound hurt or angry.

"What are you saying?" He clearly failed at trying to sound reasonable. His voice was strained and horrified.

"I don't know what I'm saying."

"Honey, you're wrong. I know what death means. I loved my parents, and I lost them."

"Davis, I'm sorry. Of course you know." She reached across the table and touched his hand.

"My leaving pushed our relationship to a place you haven't been ready to consider, but you're not going to lose me." His heart swelled with deep love for this complicated woman. He saw the fear and love in her eyes.

He pressed a kiss onto each finger. "You're right. I need the structure. If I know when I'll see you, I won't feel left hanging."

"I didn't want to tell you how hard this is for me. Dr. Z says I'm afraid to care too deeply, because I'm protecting myself against ever experiencing the pain I felt when I lost Cassie. I care deeply about you, and you're leaving." Her green eyes were filled with tears.

He understood. She was withdrawing to lessen the pain of them being apart.

"Maybe my leaving is good for us."

"Are you serious?" Her eyes had taken on the color of the turbulent waters of Puget Sound. He liked her better with a flash of anger in her eyes, not the painful look of a fragile child.

"I'll be coming back for you, Grayce Walters, every chance I get, and I'll never stop. You'll be forced to overcome your fear, because you'll realize I'm never going away."

She gave him a tremulous smile. "After Cassie's death, I learned that overcoming deep fear takes time. You can't rush it."

"We've got plenty of time. And I'm a persistent guy who will not let you go. You'll never get rid of me."

"The distance might be good for you too, Davis."

He was glad to see her color returning and the haunted look vanishing. "To make me appreciate what a wonderful woman you are."

"That, too." She gave her deep throated laugh that always turned him on.

"You'll trust that I won't betray you, even if you're not here acting like a guard dog."

He didn't want her to dissect his possessiveness. He was a male. So of course he was marking his territory.

"Guard dog—that's how you see me? I guess you might be right. But I've never felt this way about another woman. Never. And I don't expect I'll ever not be jealous of any man who looks at you. I'll still be fighting for you when we're old and gray—I'll be whacking them with my cane."

She giggled like a teenager. He wished he had known Grayce before her sister's death, before deep pain had been etched into her being.

"You look exhausted." He had been so stressed by his new position that he hadn't truly paid attention to her wan color and the dark circles under eyes, the color of crushed violets.

"I'm not sleeping well. I keep reliving my sister's death in my dreams. It's awful."

"Can't you stop the dream?" When she had explained how she processed energy in her dreams, Davis had tried to understand, but he realized he had never grasped the idea. He liked to process his energy on the slopes of Mt. Si.

"I'm working on deep fear." Her eyes started to glaze over with the haunted look again.

"There's nothing you need to be afraid of. I'll always protect you." He took her delicate hands in his powerful grasp.

"Davis, no one can protect another person from fear." There was a hint of a smile on her sumptuous lips.

"What can I do?" He hated feeling helpless.

"It would help if Angie would surface."

"Why?"

"Mrs. Hines' grief takes me back to my mother's inconsolable pain."

He understood why Grayce had become so involved trying to

help this mother. "I'll call the police and ask if there are any new leads."

"Oh, that would be great." Grayce squeezed his hand.

"I wish you hadn't got involved." She tried to pull her hand away. He tightened his grip. "I was going to say because of the toll it takes on you. I wasn't criticizing your involvement. I now understand why it's important to you to help Angie's mom. "But, I need your help, too."

"Of course. What do you need?"

Whatever shone in his eyes made Grayce get spots of color on her cheeks.

"I already helped you with your little problem this morning," she said. "Have you forgotten?"

He would never forget Grayce's lush lips around him. It was all he thought about during the long tedious meetings. Her hair brushing his thighs as her mouth... He was going to disgrace himself.

"Little? Did you just say little?" His voice was teasing. Her eyes danced back and forth.

"I've another problem," Davis continued.

"Another?" Grayce giggled again.

"Would you keep Mitzi with you while I'm in DC? I've thought about how happy she is in your office. I won't be able to take her to work, so she'd either be in my apartment or in doggie day care."

"But, Davis, she belongs with you."

"Yes, but if she's with you, I'll know she, you, and I all belong to each other."

"Davis, don't get that look. I'm not leaving until I've had my shrimp diablo."

How could he live without Grayce Walters? She always knew, before he did, what he wanted. He was about to say "let's get out of here."

CHAPTER EIGHTEEN

Brandon huddled next to Maddy on his sleeping bag. She smiled at him, and her soft, brown eyes twinkled. They were in the *jungle* on the west side of Beacon Hill above the freeway—a green belt of trees that the homeless and criminals had claimed as their own. Their group of misfits and losers hid among the homeless to prevent being tracked. Only one week before the big bang. He had started calling his mission, the big bang because it was going to be the beginning of a new and better world in which nature had equal rights with human beings, but he had to be careful not to slip.

"Brandon, what do you think?" The tight, clipped and miffed voice came from their leader Jason, the dude with the golden fleecy hair, and it rattled him back to the present.

Hell, he hadn't been listening to Jason's endless drone of "look how smart I am, look how handsome I am with my blond hair, blue eyes and seductive smile." Maddy wasn't here for the cause, she was here to sleep with Jason—as were half the women in their group. And didn't Jason know it.

Always alert to his flock, did Jason recognize his distraction?

Their leader was getting increasingly suspicious of him. Or was he only getting paranoid as the big day approached?

Jason's light eyes examined his face, searching. It was important that he not let Jason see his anxiety. Did anyone else notice his nervousness? He needed to keep his shit together. Jason was no fool.

"Sorry, Jason. I spaced out."

Maddy poked him. "Hey, this is important."

Too bad Maddy had been attracted only to Jason, or he might have spared her.

He smiled at Maddy, giving her the full-watt smile. "Sorry, Mad. You're right."

"Okay, D-day is almost here. Let's review everyone's job. Fred, you're in charge of buying the balloons. Remember, they've got to be heavy latex."

"Like my condoms, heavy latex for a heavy workout." Fred, who had terrible acne and greasy hair, was probably still a virgin. At least there was one guy in the group who was getting less than him.

"Maddy and Teresa laughed, but Erika, a hard-core feminist, rolled her eyes in disgust.

"I'll get the vegetable oil," Jason said in his usual commander-in-chief voice. He reminded Brandon of his CO in military school—always in charge, always the alpha male, and always beating the shit out of less than perfect cadets. Military school was just like home, the almighty male forcing his will on the powerless.

"I still think it's going to be tricky getting the balloons into the meeting." Erika continued to fight Jason's position as the leader. Obviously, she wasn't sleeping with him.

"Only four of us are carrying the balloons in our backpacks. Are you having trouble with my plan?"

Shit, he really wasn't up for rehashing the whole discussion of who was willing to be arrested for the cause. He had a record from his DUI and his shoplifting. He used his criminal past as an excuse for not wanting an arrest now. Maddy didn't want to be arrested because of her juvie record. He and Maddy were assigned to protest in front of Pier 69 to provide a distraction when the others entered the building. What a great irony. He wished he could laugh out loud right now and tell them he had a distraction for them.

"What's so funny, Brandon?" Jason had his eagle eye focused on him. Sweat pooled on his back and under his arms. The urge to break into a sprint seized him. He inhaled slowly, trying to move his frozen lungs. "I was just visualizing the look on the asshole commissioner's faces when you hit them with the oil."

"That's exactly my point." Erika stood. "I want to make sure the timing is right. Brandon and Maddy have to walk in with the pictures of the animals drenched in oil from the spill in the Gulf of Mexico when we belt them with the balloons filled with oil from the audience." Erika continued to give Jason shit about his plan. Same old bullshit as in all his previous groups. Always boiled down to power and sex.

"Brandon and I'll disrupt whatever they're saying when we walk into the meeting and chant "No spills in our waters," Maddy said.

"And when the audience turns back toward Maddy and Brandon, we'll stand and throw."

"Tom and Susan are going to this Tuesday's meeting to check out the space."

Tom and Susan were the only non-misfits of the group. From wealthy East Coast families, they came to college together and got radicalized in environmental issues at liberal Evergreen College. North Face jackets and expensive haircuts, they both looked and acted as if they could just as likely be working in corporate America as hatching illegal ecoterrorist plots. Except for Maddy, the entire group had been at Evergreen with Jason. How Maddy had met Jason remained a mystery.

"Wherever we sit, we've got to nail the president and three commissioners," Jason said.

Teresa stood and addressed the group in a grave voice. "I'll be in the front row, ready to record the entire proceedings, the surprise attack and the arrest, then immediately post on the Internet. We want the pictures of the oil-soaked commissioners to be front page on national news."

"Any questions?" Jason looked at each person.

Was Jason suspicious? Jason seemed to be watching. Hell, he was getting paranoid. Only seven more days.

"Everyone stay low. And only communicate on the World of Warfare site. We'll meet in two days under the Ballard Bridge."

CHAPTER NINETEEN

Grayce sat at her desk and recorded observations about the aging Golden Retriever she had just treated. Both she and the owner were grateful that acupuncture was relieving the pain of Blue's arthritic spine.

She heard a male voice and the sound of canine nails on the wood floor. She glanced at her schedule to make sure she had no more appointments. She was blocked out for the afternoon since she was holding a clinic for veterinarians on the use of acupuncture in the emergency room setting.

She had developed different training sessions to keep her clinical skills current and to interact with her colleagues. She had no idea how in demand she would become. Her clinics were immediately filled. Everyone wanted her to do more, but she had limited the clinics to every three months. Now, with Davis leaving, she'd have more time to run clinics. The thought depressed her.

She heard Hollie's laughter. James must have appeared, although he avoided coming to the office. Intrigued by the mystery guest, she walked to the door. Sergeant Welby leaned over Hollie's computer.

Hollie didn't allow anyone behind her desk, and no one touched her computer.

"I had no idea that this site existed," Sergeant Welby said, resting one bronzed hand on Hollie's shoulder as they both gazed at her computer screen

Mitzi was stretched on her side, her long body pressed against Talley, who had positioned herself in front of Hollie's desk. Grayce was always impressed by Mitzi's intuitive healing of the wounded animals who came to the office.

Sergeant Welby whipped around quickly when Grayce opened the door. The hyper-vigilant solider moved closer to Hollie as if to protect her from the intruder.

"Sergeant Welby?" Grayce couldn't contain her surprise.

The young soldier, dressed in a white t-shirt that hugged his muscular body and snug blue jeans, was a very attractive man. He had a tattoo of blue stars across his upper arm. Grayce intuitively recognized the sergeant's loss.

"You don't have an appointment today, do you?"

A flush of color crept up the young man's weather-beaten neck into his face. He came around from behind the desk. "Talley and I were in the neighborhood and thought we'd stop by. I hope that isn't a problem, ma'am."

Grayce felt like the ogre in a fairy tale about star-crossed lovers. "You and Talley are always welcome. I hope you'll come whenever you're in the neighborhood." Sergeant Welby lived a good hour's drive from Seattle.

Hollie stood, almost bumping into the sergeant. They both moved at the same time to avoid each other.

Grayce wanted to laugh at their comic discomfort, but she wouldn't embarrass Hollie.

"Sergeant Welby..." Hollie looked at Grayce. Patches of color shone through her pale make-up.

"You're to call me Nick," he said, his voice lowered. Nick stared at Hollie, who was dressed in her feminine white dress, without her usual combat boots. The choice might have been practical since the temperature was hitting 85 degrees—absolutely sweltering for Seattleites.

Hollie turned her face, her dark lashes covering her eyes and her feelings. "Nick plays *World of Warfare*. I was showing him a site a friend of mine developed. I'm sorry if we disturbed you. I know you have to teach this afternoon."

Nick was a very virile young man, and that combined with his obvious love for Talley and skill at *World of Warfare* had sealed the deal. He was allowed into Hollie's space.

"You didn't interrupt me." As if her office didn't have endless interruptions. "I was worried that I missed someone on the schedule."

Mitzi continued to lean against Talley who had sat up attentively when Grayce came into the outer office. Grayce bent and petted Talley. "How's my girl? You look rested."

With her owner enjoying a courtly interaction with a beautiful young woman, Talley had relaxed.

"We swim after our run in the morning. And we swim in the evening. Seems to help both of us sleep better.'

Nick's face flushed bright red. She watched him watch Hollie. It didn't take an intuitive to see that he had been fantasizing about Hollie at night.

"I'm glad that you're both enjoying the swimming." Nick and Talley needed a disciplined regimen.

Hollie said, "I didn't want to disturb you when you were preparing your notes. I've a brilliant idea about Maddy's t-shirt."

Hollie angled her head toward Nick, asking whether she should share.

Grayce turned toward Nick. "We're trying to help locate a missing Marine and her friend." Nick might have a new perspective, since he had been a solider in Afghanistan.

"Are you talking about the Teen Feed t-shirt?"

"I can enlarge it and do a Google reverse search," Hollie said.

Nick's smile widened. His eyes fixed on Hollie's animated face.

Seen through Nick's appreciative eyes, Hollie was a stunning beauty, as James had said the first time he met her.

"Back up. What picture?"

Like a sunflower in search of sunshine, Nick leaned toward Hollie and her vibrant glow.

It was going to be a long summer watching these two fall in love, especially with Davis leaving. "Hollie, what picture?" Grayce asked.

"Remember when James was disgusted with Maddy's t-shirt. It's a *World of Warfare* customized t-shirt."

Unaware of Nick's total absorption, Hollie excitedly explained to Grayce. When she looked at Nick, whatever she saw in his face, made her stopped midsentence.

"So?"

"It's brilliant." Nick's voice was filled with wonder as if Hollie had just discovered the rules of gravity.

Hollie's almond eyes grew round, and she touched her tongue to her lip.

Grayce heard the hitch in Nick's breathing.

A really long summer.

"Hollie might be able to find the person who designed the t-shirt by downloading the image to Google." Nick looked at Grayce.

"I didn't know you could do such a thing," Grayce said.

"It's alright, boss, you know a lot of other things."

Now she definitely felt like an old, fifth wheel.

"Can you give me the picture from Angie's mom? I can take it over to Kinko's to enlarge and then download the image while you're teaching."

"Talley and I can walk with you to copy the picture." Nick looked longingly at Hollie.

Hollie looked shyly down at her non-booted feet and shrugged. "If you want to."

"Once we identify the designer of the t-shirt, we could look for her or him on the *World of Warfare* chat rooms—monitor their chatter," Nick said.

"That's brilliant, Nick." Hollie smiled, her whole face gleaming.

"You would've thought of it eventually." Nick gave a wide grin, looking very young and very handsome.

Hollie turned with a gasp. "Boss, you've got to get going or you'll be late."

Grayce couldn't remember exactly when Hollie had taken total charge of her schedule. Grayce, not gifted with punctuality, now relied completely on the young woman to manage her time.

"You never know what traffic will be like on I-5."

"You're right. I'd better go."

"I forgot..." Hollie looked at Nick and stammered. "I forgot in all the excitement." Hollie never stammered. She looked young and hesitant. Grayce's heart expanded with joy for the young woman.

"Louise Marley called you. She hopes you can come down and see Frank."

"Louise Marley, the movie star?" Nick looked at Grayce with a new appreciation. Maybe he thought she was hip after all.

"Dr. Walters treats her schnauzer. She wanted Dr. Walters to become a Hollywood vet, but she wouldn't leave Seattle." Grayce was always touched by Hollie's admiration.

"Is Frank sick?"

"She told me she was tempted to lie, but Frank isn't sick. She just wants you to come down and visit."

Grayce had been thinking of a trip to LA after Davis left. She had a special connection with Louise Marley. She felt as close to her as a sister. She and Louise could discuss the men who left them. According to the tabloids, Louise was dating a bad boy musician. She hoped not. The guy was known for the string of heartbreaks he left in his wake.

Grayce returned to her desk to finish one last note before she left for the clinic. She missed not having Mitzi in the office. Her companion was spending the day with Davis because of Grayce's afternoon teaching commitment. Grayce loved Mitzi's calm presence and even breathing in the background as she completed her charting.

A woman's voice called from the outer office. "Anyone here? Dr. Walters?"

Grayce didn't recognized the voice. She stood and walked to the door.

A tall, muscular woman with jet-black hair, in blue jeans and a dark blue t-shirt, held a large bouquet of red roses. "Dr. Walters?"

The woman looked familiar to Grayce. With the Marine Corp's motto, "Semper Fidelis," written in bold white letters across her t-shirt, Grayce recognized her surprise visitor.

"Angie? Angie Hines?" Grayce clasped her hands together in delight.

"Yes, ma'am."

Grayce curbed the urge to wrap her arms around the somber woman. Angie Hines, like Hollie, wouldn't be open to uninvited touch or hugs.

"I'm so glad you're back."

"Thank you, ma'am."

"Did your brother find you?"

"A woman identified my picture from the posters that Hunter had put up in the University District and notified the police. The police found me on Brooklyn Street."

"This makes my day." Grayce repressed all the questions she wanted to ask. The biggest question was what had prevented Angie from returning to her family.

"I wanted to come and thank you in person. My mom told me that your help was huge. Hunter and the police were able to focus their search in the University District because of you."

"I didn't do that much. It was Ossie. She wouldn't leave your Teen Feed t-shirt alone."

"The crazy part—that-shirt isn't mine. It belongs to my friend."

"Well, no matter. I'm glad you're safely back. Your mother must be so relieved."

"She is." She handed Grayce the bouquet of vibrant roses. "These are for you."

The price tag was still on the plastic wrap.

"They're beautiful. You didn't have to get me anything, but thank you." Grayce gestured to the open door. "Please come into my office."

"I don't want to disturb you."

"Not at all. I've got to leave in a few minutes, but let's chat."

Angie nodded and followed Grayce into her office.

Grayce found a vase under the sink and filled it with water. She carried the vase with the flowers to her desk.

"Please sit down." Grayce pointed to the chair across from her desk. "I'm sorry your mom didn't come."

"I needed to do a lot of fast talking to convince her not to come today." Angie rubbed her face then crossed her arms in an anxious, tic-like manner. "I didn't want my mom here, because I needed to talk with you alone." Angie shifted to one side of the chair. "My mother will be upset when she learns about my plans. I'm going to continue to look for my friend."

"For Maddy?" Grayce tried to keep her tone neutral, but knew she had an edge of pique. Did Angie not realize what she had put her mother through?

"You know about Maddy?"

"Yes, your mom shared that you were looking for Maddy when you disappeared. Do you have any idea where she might be?"

"No, I'm not sure, but I know I was close to finding her when I blanked out."

"Blanked out?" Grayce asked.

"I hit my head. I still have a big bump." Angie rubbed her hand along the base of her skull. "My psychiatrist believes the head trauma triggered my PTSD and my subsequent loss of memory. I don't remember where I was during the entire time I was missing."

Grayce caught herself, pressing her lips into a tight line in an effort to control her response. "How absolutely frightening. Does your doctor think it's wise to resume your search?" With dark circles and a nervous twitch above her eyes, Angie didn't look ready to go back on the street.

Angie's long eyelashes fluttered shut. She gnawed her lower lip, looking a great deal less certain. "I haven't told anyone about my plans. I have a vague memory, more like a sensation, that I was very close to finding Maddy before I was injured. I hoped that you would use your skills to help me."

Grayce felt as if someone raked their nails down her spine or she had run into an electric fence. "I'm a veterinarian, not a detective. I don't really know how to locate missing people."

"But look how you helped to find me."

"Why not get the police involved? They're the ones who found you." Grayce wanted to say why not your brother, but this wasn't the time to go off on that mystery.

"I can't go to the police. If Maddy is back using and is found by the police..." Angie shook her head. "It would ruin her military career. Maddy has fought against all odds to succeed as a Marine, and I don't want her career destroyed."

"I really respect your commitment to finding your friend. I know you served together in Afghanistan."

"Marines don't give up on each other. Maddy is trying to numb herself from her demons from the war. I've got to help her, get her back to our treatment group."

"Why don't you ask your brother? He's seems very skilled at this kind of thing."

"My step-brother and I aren't close. I want to protect Maddy's privacy after all she's been through. I don't know what condition I'll find her in."

Grayce didn't miss that Angie avoided sharing any further information about Hunter.

"Ma'am. I wouldn't ask if it were for me, but Maddy is one hell of a Marine."

How could Grayce say no to a Marine who wanted to save another battle-scarred veteran? Angie had to be terrified that, back on the street, she might relapse. Grayce couldn't let her go alone on the dangerous streets.

"My mom told me that you solved your last case with the help of a French Poodle. I'm hoping you and your poodle could help me search the *jungle* in Seattle."

Grayce's stomach felt like she'd done a belly flop smack off a high board. "The *jungle*?" Her recurring nightmares of being lost in the jungle zoomed though her mind.

"The *jungle* is the green belt on the west slope of Beacon Hill."

Alarm galloped into her stomach.

"Is there a reason why you specifically want to look there?"

"Before I got amnesia, I had been searching in the homeless encampments and I never made it there. And with Maddy's ranger skills, I think it'd be an easy place for her to hide."

"Mitzi and I'll help you look for Maddy. I want to help. I appreciate what you both did for our country. I need to leave for my course, but call me tomorrow and we'll work out when Mitzi and I can go with you."

Angie stood. Her lips curved in the first smile of the visit. "Thank you, Dr. Walters. I knew I could depend on you."

Grayce wished she could be as happy as Angie about her decision. Her sixth sense was humming and not in a good way.

CHAPTER TWENTY

Without Davis, but with flowers, champagne, and Mitzi, Grayce waited to meet his sisters for the first time. Her stomach somersaulted when she pressed the doorbell of the massive Georgian brick house in the Mount Baker neighborhood.

The children's toys and clothing scattered across the grass and the butterscotch-colored cat asleep in the bushes helped to soften the house's austere façade and calm her nervousness. Mitzi barked at a child's high-pitched shriek from inside the house.

Grayce wished she could muster Mitzi's enthusiasm about the dinner with Davis' sisters and families. It would've been easier if she and Davis could have arrived together. He got delayed in a meeting in Bremerton at the nuclear submarine base. He had texted her that he would meet her at his sister's house.

She took a slow, deep breath. She was going to enjoy tonight and celebrate the great news that Angie had been found.

Jane, in a stained apron, opened the door. Her black hair, high cheekbones and blue eyes perfectly matched the features of her older brother. She also shared the same dimple in her chin.

"Grayce, we're so glad you've come. Davis just called me to say he's on his way. I'm Jane and this is Lindsay."

A small child hid behind her mother's leg as her older, dark-haired brother ran to the door. His eager shouts echoed in the formal foyer. "Mitzi's here."

Mitzi sat as three children raced toward her and began to pet and hug her. Mitzi sat patiently, enduring the affectionate grasps and pulls.

Another of Davis' look-alike sisters joined the boisterous group. "I'm Helene and this is Emma." A fat cherub with her fingers threaded through her mother's hair watched Grayce with big blue eyes. It was obvious that the Davis family gene pool was potent.

Jane pointed to the children. "Grayce, this is Gray, Trevor, and Mackenzie."

Mackenzie, dressed in cowboy boots and a pink tutu, showed Grayce her finger. "I have an owie. Do you want to see?"

Grayce bent to inspect a tiny scratch on the girl's index finger. "That must hurt."

The smaller of the two boys showed Grayce his knee. "Gray knocked me down. But it doesn't hurt."

Jane laughed. "I guess animals aren't the only ones who recognize your healing abilities."

Gray tugged on his mother's sleeve. "Can we take Mitzi in the back yard?"

"What a great idea. It will give our guest time to adjust to her welcome," Jane said, with a smile and wink at Grayce.

The children gave her a mere glimpse as they rushed toward the back door with Mitzi in the middle. She could hear Mackenzie exclaim, "Let's throw Mitzi the ball. She loves to catch balls."

She handed Jane the wine and flowers. "Thank you for inviting me."

Jane leaned down for Lindsay to smell the lilies Grayce had brought. "You might want to take your presents back after you've been here a while."

She smiled, not sure if Helene was kidding.

There was an uncanny resemblance between Jane's and Davis' smile. "It isn't exactly a restful event, but Davis said that you've braved dinner with Aunt Aideen. We love our Aunt, but... she has never stopped being a 60s hippie."

Both women laughed. "Did she read your tarot or your palm?" Jane asked.

"She can be terrifying when she gets mad. She intimidates everyone," Helene said.

Helene had it wrong. Grayce had felt an immediate connection with Aunt Aideen. Aunt Aideen's prediction about Hunter had been wrong, he hadn't embroiled Grayce in anything dangerous. She and Aunt Aideen were kindred spirits despite their different styles.

"Let's open the champagne to fortify you for the upcoming family dinner."

"Great idea, Helene." Jane pointed at Helene. "She's the smart one of the family."

The sisters smiled at the inside joke.

Grayce stood in the middle of the sunny kitchen. The sisters' chatter enveloped her in kindness. Grayce experienced a yearning for sisterly intimacy like what she would've had with Cassie.

"I don't think we've ever had anyone for dinner the day she's made a splash in *The Seattle Times*." Jane wrapped a towel around the champagne bottle. Helene handed Grayce the coupe glasses.

"You don't look any older than your graduation picture from Cornell. Are you from the East Coast?" Jane asked.

Grayce's stomach started the same sensation of falling from a great distance.

Jane turned to put Lindsay into her high chair. "I thought Davis said you grew up in Seattle."

"I don't think Grayce knows what we're talking about. You know you're in today's newspaper?" Helene turned toward Grayce as she placed Emma into a seat that was attached to the counter.

"No." Her voice came out tremulous.

Her voice must have betrayed her shock. Both sisters stopped at the same time and gawked at her.

"I was in the clinic all day," Grayce said.

"Davis didn't tell you?" Jane asked.

"It's just like him," Helene chimed.

The sisters exchanged a knowing look. What had Davis done?

Helene walked to the long kitchen table scattered with markers, papers, dolls and half-eaten sandwiches. The newspaper sat on top of the heap. "Grayce, come sit here while I open the champagne."

Grayce lowered herself to the chair after she removed a single striped sock. Her eyes focused on the paper. *Dr. Grayce Walters* was the caption under a very large picture of her from the award banquet at Cornell.

Her heart raced, thundering against her chest. The headlines read "Animal Acupuncturist Works with Cat to Find Missing Woman Veteran." Her gifts were exposed in big black and white bold letters.

She couldn't focus. Her hands shook when she lifted the paper.

Emily Chow had done her homework. The newscaster had shared all the details of her training, her awards, her studies in China and her practice as an animal acupuncturist. She gulped her champagne. She couldn't breathe.

Helene poured more champagne into her glass. "It looks as if you need this."

She stared up into a pair of eyes that were identical to Davis'.

Helene sat down and patted her hand. "This came as a surprise?"

She nodded.

"I'm not trying to intrude, but it's obvious that the article has upset you. Jane and I are truly sorry for our cavalier way of announcing it. We had no idea."

"It's...well, it's so out there for anyone and everyone to know."

"And you didn't want people to know?"

She took another sip of champagne. "I guess that doesn't matter anymore."

"You're not really interested in public acclaim." Helene understood more than she wanted her to.

"I'm a pretty private person. At least James and Hollie will be happy."

What was it about the Davis family that made her feel as if she wanted to unload her burdens?

"Seattle is an animal lovers' city, so I don't think anyone is going to stalk you from this article. And it can't hurt your practice to get publicity."

Grayce heard Davis' voice at the front door. "Where is everyone?" He walked into the kitchen and a rush of conflicting emotions overwhelmed her. Was it just this morning they had been in bed?

"Champagne? What are we celebrating?" Davis hugged Jane, who stopped her chopping and pointed her heavy knife at Davis.

"You've got some explaining to do..."

"What have I done now?"

Helene walked toward her brother. "I'm sure you meant it to be a surprise. Come on, Jane. We'll let big brother get himself out of this one."

The sisters gathered their infants and left the kitchen.

"What the hell are those two talking about?"

Davis' sisters weren't intimidated by their massive brother. And they were acting very protective of Grayce. As she was leaving the kitchen, Helene turned and smiled at Grayce. A warm rush of belonging eased Grayce's stress.

Davis bent and kissed her on the lips. "What are my crazy sisters talking about?"

"The article in the newspaper."

"Article in the newspaper? Why should an article in the newspaper upset my sisters?"

"They were referring to the story about me."

"You're in the paper?"

The warmth in the kitchen suddenly cooled. Grayce was offended by the smooth way Davis pretended not to know.

"This." She pointed to the paper spread among the junk.

Davis leaned toward the paper. "I had no idea. I've been in Bremerton all day."

"If you didn't know, how come you're quoted?"

"Let me see that." He took the paper and read. "That's my quote from last year's wharf fire. I had no idea." When he was finished, he sat down and took her hand. "Are you okay?"

"It's a shock to see my name and picture blazing across the paper."

"Grayce, I'm sorry, but you did really help to find Angie." Davis squeezed her hand. "I know how much you hate the scrutiny."

She leaned toward him. "It's okay. It's not the end of the world. And as I told your sisters, Hollie and James will be thrilled."

"What about you, Grayce, are you happy?" He got that special gleam in his cornflower blue eyes—the one that she found irresistible.

She tugged on Davis' hand, bringing him closer to her face. "You know I am." She watched his bright eyes darken with desire. "I'm..." She licked her lips slowly, tantalizing. She heard the hitch in Davis' breath. She giggled and stood up. "I'm famous in Seattle."

"What? You little minx. Come here." Davis stood to grab her as she tried to rush past him. He caught her in his arms and pressed her against the table.

"I think you need to learn a lesson on respecting your elders."

She couldn't help but giggle. The champagne must have gone to her head. Davis swallowed her giggle with his voracious lips. She forgot all about the newspaper and her location until she heard a child shout.

"Mom, Uncle Ewan is kissing Mitzi's mother."

CHAPTER TWENTY-ONE

Grayce, Davis and Mitzi headed home from the party. The sky was tinged orange in the west—and very soon fireworks would start erupting in Elliot Bay. On the back seat of Grayce's beat-up Subaru, Mitzi slept deeply. Entertaining five children had exhausted the poodle.

"Wasn't I smart to use the light rail so I could get you to drive me home?" Davis' voice thickened as his fingers wandered under her skirt.

Davis had disrupted her plan to check out the *jungle* on the west side of Beacon Hill on her drive home. She decided to take the Beacon Hill route anyway and then jump on 99. Davis wasn't paying any attention to her route home, since he was intent on his exploration.

"Not while I'm driving." Her words came out breathless with the progression of his roving fingers.

Davis was very capable of multi-tasking. As he talked, his fingers advanced in slow circles on her inner thigh. "I can't believe you worried about meeting my sisters. I told you that you would impress them and that all my nephews and nieces would love you instantly."

"Davis, stop." Grayce grabbed his hand.

"We're going to have our own fireworks when I get you home." His voice was gruff.

She drove down the curved, steep western hill. At night, the *jungle* looked ominous. Her heart sped in tandem with her descent into the dark night. "I liked your family. They're great."

Watching Davis play with his nieces and nephews added one more attractive layer to this complicated man. He had won her respect with his gentle and concerned treatment of Mitzi, but she had no idea how much more she could love this man until she saw his tender care of his nephews and nieces in his arms. He just kept getting better.

"Mackenzie followed you around all evening. And little Emma climbed into your lap and fell asleep," Davis said.

Grayce had cherished the feel of the toddler in her arms. At some point, she wanted children, but until now, the reality had been far removed from her present life. Now, with Davis as a partner, she began to believe in the possibility of a life filled with children and Davis.

"The chief wants me to attend a conference in DC this week. I'm going to fly out on the red-eye on Wednesday."

Her joyful fantasy of a home filled with children disappeared in a flash. "That was sudden."

"There is a whole procedure for getting my security clearance with the FBI. Zac, you remember him, right? The guy from the FBI that helped me with my investigation. He's arranged a special tour of the J. Edgar Hoover building."

Grayce heard the excitement in his voice and felt a hollow ache building in her chest.

"And I have to find an apartment since there won't be a lot of time once I get started on the job."

"You'll be working long hours?"

"Probably, but I like a challenge."

Davis was focused and driven, and once he got involved with

national security issues, she wasn't sure he'd be happy to return to his mundane life in Seattle.

"I've got a realtor looking for an apartment in the Adams Morgan neighborhood. It has a great feel—a small village in North-west DC, great restaurants, all in walking distance. You're going to love it."

She didn't say it didn't matter if she loved it since she wouldn't be there much. Her heart wasn't breaking, but she had been fooling herself. Davis out of her daily life was going to hurt. She managed to give a half-hearted reply. "Sounds great, Davis."

"I've booked the flight home for Saturday night. Will you pick me up?"

"You know I will."

"Honey, what is it? I won't let this job come between us? You know that, right?"

Her intuition wasn't working around Davis. It was clouded with her own sense of loss. Davis had good intentions, but once he got focused on his work, would he have time or energy for them? Men easily compartmentalized their lives.

"I'm just tired. There has been a lot going on. With the news-paper article and meeting your family, I haven't had a chance yet to tell you about who came to my office."

"Who?" Davis asked.

"Angie Hines."

"The missing woman? She came to see you? Why?"

"To thank me for supporting her mom while she was missing. She brought me flowers." Grayce omitted that Angie remained upset and agitated. If Davis perceived that Angie wasn't fully recovered, his bonfire temper would ignite.

Grayce pulled her car into a parking spot in front of Davis' condo and turned toward Davis. "Angie's a very strong woman. She reminds me of Toni from the fire department's holiday party."

"Really?" Davis' voice sounded strained. He never discussed his past with Toni, and Grayce never asked.

"Not the seductive part that you liked." She ran her finger along his hand that rested on her thigh.

"You know I never...was with Toni?"

"It doesn't matter, and I was teasing."

He leaned forward and rubbed his lips against hers. "I like teasing." His wolfish eyes gleamed in the streetlights.

"Angie has the same warrior attitude as Toni, as if she'd be willing take anyone on and take them down."

"Where has Angie been all this time?"

"She doesn't remember. She had a head injury that triggered amnesia. That's her psychiatrist's theory. He told her it's not uncommon for people with PTSD to disassociate from any memories around a new trauma."

"At first, she didn't recognize her mother. Angie gradually recovered her memory by returning to her apartment and to Ossie. I've read some articles about amnesia. There are surprising triggers for what can bring back a person's memory—a familiar setting or a familiar song. Of course, I believe being with Ossie helped her."

"I'm sure you comforted her." He reached over and pulled her close to him and whispered, "Honey, why are we still sitting in the car?"

"You're not going to like the decision I've made. We both may need time alone to calm down."

"You mean I'm going to get mad, and you won't want to stay overnight with me?"

Grayce nodded. "You could surprise me and not get mad."

Davis released her. "You better tell me."

"Angie asked for my help."

"What kind of help?"

"She asked me to help her find her friend, Maddy."

"Go on." His voice was level and even. Never a good sign when Davis was trying to appear in control.

"She asked if Mitzi and I could go to the green belt on Beacon Hill to search for Maddy."

The passing car lights kept flashing on Davis' extraordinary, angular face. The suffused light made his profile harsh and formidable.

"What the f..." He hardly ever used the "f" word.

"An experienced Marine wants your help in finding a drug addict?"

"Maddy is her friend, a fellow Marine."

"You're a goddamn acupuncturist, not a detective." He let out an exasperated breath. "When does it stop, Grayce? People asking for your help. I got that you wanted to help the mother. But now you're helping a Marine with PTSD?"

"I like helping people."

"By going to one of the roughest parts of town?" He angled his body, looming over her. "Dead bodies show up over there. And how is this related to your work with animals?"

His sarcasm tainted the space between them.

"We have a police department to help Angie find her friend," he added.

"Angie is trying to protect Maddy from the police. If Maddy is back doing drugs, it will ruin her military career."

"But why ask you? Doesn't she have Marine friends who could help?"

"Emily Chow told her that Mitzi and I had helped in your case. Angie's mother has complete faith that I could help."

"I'd like to kill that woman."

"Mrs. Hines?"

"Emily Chow. All for a story to advance her own career, she's got you involved in a mess."

"I don't think helping a desperate woman is a mess. Angie said Maddy was like her kid sister." She was losing her patience with Davis. "I didn't find Angie, but the police knew where to look because of my visit to Teen Feed."

Davis linked his fingers between hers. "I'm sorry. Of course you helped."

"I don't see any harm if Angie, Mitzi, and I walk through the area during the day." Grayce chose not to disclose that she had been dreaming about the *jungle* and knew from her dreams that she was supposed to go.

Davis squeezed her hand. "What if Angie has a PTSD flashback and thinks you're the Taliban?"

Angie would never harm her. How could she explain to Davis her understanding of people?

"You're kidding, right?"

"No. Yes. Hell, I don't know. You're driving me crazy, Grayce. It's hard enough to leave you, but to think about you putting yourself in danger."

"Davis, remember our discussion about your need to do dangerous work? This is no different. I hate the idea of you taking risks."

"I'm trained for danger, you're not."

"But I am--"

"No, you're not."

She'd hoped to avoid this discussion with him. She couldn't explain how she knew when she was in synchrony with her dreams and had to follow the path of deep knowing.

"I know I'm not trained the way you are, but I've got other unseen abilities. I can help people, and I can't withhold my assistance from those in need. I understand your need to protect me. I do, but you've got to have faith that I have good judgment."

"I'm not saying you don't have good judgment. I have a different perspective on the evil out there."

Grayce leaned over and kissed him on the cheek. "I'm so proud of us. We're actually having a discussion."

"I have an ulterior motive. Can we go inside to further discuss our dangerous work?"

"Really? You're not going to go all Attila the Hun about me being a weak female."

"I promise not to go Attila until we're in the bed."

Grayce laughed. How could she not love this man?

––––––––––

Davis held Grayce in his arms. She slept deeply. He couldn't sleep. Grayce Walters was harmful to his health. He had become an obsessed man. It was absurd. He wanted to shelter her, never let her be in danger.

For years, he had made jokes about his friends when they fell in love, but if his friends could see him now, how they would enjoy his torment.

Grayce sighed and buried her face on his chest. She was so soft and tiny, her bones like bird wings. Although small, Grayce was no pushover. When she wasn't pleased, she got the same look as his Aunt Aideen. Her green eyes turned a deeper shade, a turbulent green. She was like his aunt—not in size or demeanor, but in her emotional strength.

He had to avoid playing the macho man role. Grayce had been impressed with his rational behavior. His only request was that she take James with her to Beacon Hill. She had been offended by the idea of her needing a man to protect her, but she didn't understand male instincts. James knew how to handle himself in a fight. It was a testosterone thing.

"What am I going to do with you, my little warrior?" he whispered. "I'm drowning over here, Grayce. Help me." She hadn't heard a word he said. She might not like him acting all primitive in her life, but she definitely liked him as Attila in bed.

CHAPTER TWENTY-TWO

Brandon sat away from the cameras in the public library. There were no unmonitored spaces anymore. He was vigilant in avoiding the cameras—always turned away from their prying lens. They'd be looking for him soon, reviewing surveillance tapes. There were much weirder homeless dudes who deserved the camera time. He'd let them draw Big Brother's attention.

Protected by his hoody pulled over his hair, sunglasses, and beard, he settled into a soft chair and opened *The Seattle Times*. Nothing of importance. More boring shit about Boeing. He reached for the local news section. Boeing would be old news in less than five days' time, and his face would be plastered on the front page.

It was too bad that he'd miss the spectacle of his father Frank's face contorted with the familiar purple eggplant rage and his mother Meryl's facelift sag in disappointment. His stomach lurched as he flashed on the memory of his mother's red fingernails, sparkling with her giant diamonds, squeezing his arm, cajoling him to prove to his father that he could excel. His parents would both get their wish—their loser son would make them famous.

They wouldn't be able to escape the notoriety. The experts

would analyze how they, the perfect couple, had fucked up. They'd try to hide at their place on San Juan Island, but everyone would know.

From his little cabin on the remote west side of Kapas Island, he'd enjoy reading the theories of his downward spiral despite his affluent background and doting parents. He'd never see them again since he'd be heading to Jakarta. Courtesy of Boeing. On Malaysian Airlines. He hoped the airlines had its shit together by then. He doubted Frank and Meryl would miss him.

He gasped as he stared at the newspaper. He recognized the woman's picture under the heading. "Animal Acupuncturist Works with Cat to Find Missing Woman Veteran."

The meddling blond bitch from the house on 65th. Her picture was featured on the local news section. She smiled at the camera, accepting an award from Cornell. Of course the bitch went to an Ivy League school and won awards. Rage boiled up into his gullet. And she had found Maddy's friend. He wouldn't let her interfere in his carefully constructed plans. She was too close. She wouldn't get any closer.

His hands shook. He'd make sure of it.

CHAPTER TWENTY-THREE

G rayce, James and Mitzi waited for Angie by the dirt track that led down to the west side of Beacon Hill. They met at sunrise since Hollie had told them they had to arrive either in the early morning or late at night to find people at their spots. Grayce had chosen sunrise since Hollie had warned them that the safety risks significantly escalated at nighttime.

"You got me up before sunrise and didn't have an espresso or a *pain au chocolat* waiting for me in the car," James whined in an affected singsong. "And now you tell me I can't talk about fashion or sex. What will I talk about?"

"Angie's been through hell and is worried about her friend."

"And from her picture, Angie would benefit from my fashion advice. She'd look a lot better without all the hair."

"You're here at my invitation, so no fashion or risqué comments to Angie."

"You mean at Davis' coercion. Did Davis know that you planned to muzzle me?"

"No, but I'm sure he'd agree."

"I love that the hulk admires my fighting powers. Who said the moon isn't made of brie?"

"He said that you'd be good in a fight."

"James' voice lowered an octave into that range that meant serious. "I only use my martial arts for self-defense; but, I've done a lot of that. They're sharp." James wasn't talking only about the high school bullies, but about his father.

"There's Angie," Grayce said.

Mitzi stood when she saw Angie marching toward them with a backpack and a soldier's stiff bearing. She was dressed in old military clothes—fatigue pants, boots and a white t-shirt. Her thick, black hair was pulled back in a ponytail.

"OMG, I'm in a GI Joe movie. How far are we walking? I'm not staying overnight, no matter what Davis said."

"My God, James. Calm down. We're not going far."

"I wish I'd thought to wear my fatigue jeans. She looks so apropos."

"And I'm sure Angie dressed to make a fashion statement while searching for her friend in homeless camps."

"Dr. Walters, thank you for coming." Angie stood at attention.

"Angie, please call me Grayce."

"Yes, ma'am."

"And this is James, and this is Mitzi."

James extended his hand. "The pleasure is all mine, Angie."

"Thank you, sir." Grayce was never going to admit that James' presence was a compromise with her over-protective boyfriend.

"Hi, Mitzi." Angie squatted on her knees to pet the poodle. "We didn't have any poodles working in Afghanistan."

"Their haircuts are hard to maintain in the sand," James said in his usual sardonic tone.

Grayce elbowed him square in the ribs.

Angie looked up at James in his tight, black jeans, black polo shirt, and expensive Montblanc watch. "You might be right, sir." Her face remained inscrutable.

Angie rubbed the soft fur on Mitzi's head. "You ready to work, girl?"

Grayce didn't want to disappoint Angie by telling her that Mitzi wasn't a working dog.

"I walked through the north side of the hill yesterday and didn't find anything. I thought we'd walk toward the south. I'm hoping Mitzi can lead us."

"You do realize that Mitzi isn't trained for this sort of thing," Grayce said.

"Yes, ma'am. I'm aware that a poodle isn't a search and rescue dog, but I'm hoping Mitzi's instincts will take over."

"Let's give her a try. Mitzi is a remarkable dog. I'll let her off her leash."

"Yes, ma'am."

"Angie, it's going to be a long day if you keep ma'aming me. Please call me Grayce."

"Yes, ma...I mean Grayce."

With her lead off, Mitzi bounded down the hill, following the dirt path. Grayce felt trepidation as they started their descent. She hadn't had any nightmares in anticipation of today, but she was wary of what the suffering of the homeless might arouse.

"I'll walk point. Sir, can you take the rear?"

James snickered and said under his breath, "If you only knew, honey."

"Sir?"

"Nothing, Angie. Just muttering to myself."

Grayce was impressed that James didn't make any further suggestive comments.

They followed the trail as it twisted along the trees. The roar of I-5 droned below the hill. They walked in silence as Mitzi ran ahead with her nose to the ground. Frequently the poodle would check back to make sure they were following. Grayce felt like she was doing a military reconnaissance.

Grayce and Mitzi had worked together on the wharf investigations, then she became the nurturing office dog. Now the poodle had been transformed into a working police dog. Was there anything Mitzi couldn't do?

Mitzi led them to the first encampment. It was deserted. An empty refrigerator box with Frigidaire printed on the outside provided shelter. The box had one plastic bag filled with what looked like old clothing. Nothing of any value could be left since it would have been stolen.

"Frigidaire. A dependable choice. I might use them on my next project." James stood to one side of the box, pretending to analyze it as Mitzi sniffed the area around the box. "Cardboard wouldn't be the material I'd choose. Not exactly weather resistant."

"No, sir. I don't believe it is. But it will give a person temporary shelter."

James dealt with uncomfortable emotions with cynical humor, but Grayce wasn't sure if Angie was getting James' humor or that she felt she had to humor him.

Mitzi yelped at them and hurried down the path.

"Guess that means we should follow," Angie said.

The sun hadn't come over Beacon Hill yet, so they walked in the shadows and cold air. Grayce didn't want to think about what it would be like hiding in the trees, trying to stay warm and safe every night.

They walked for at least ten minutes.

"Are we in Tacoma yet?" James asked.

"No, sir. I believe this green belt ends around Michigan Avenue."

Grayce would've liked to tell James to stop baiting Angie but knew from experience that would only increase James' performance.

"Grayce didn't bring me an espresso, even though she knows how crabby I get if I don't have my morning fix."

"I brought some rations, sir. If you'd like chocolate, I've got a candy bar."

"I only eat Theo's or Dilettante chocolate."

"Sorry, sir. It's a Snickers."

"What else you carrying in your pack? By the way, I like how it matches your pants. Very chic-chic."

"James..." Grayce started and then stopped. Angie had survived Afghanistan, she could survive James.

"They're military issue, sir."

Or maybe not.

"Angie, honey. You have to stop calling me 'sir' unless you call me Sir James." James flicked his hand in the air. "Sir James sounds like a rapper. Never mind. Just call me James."

"Yes, sir. I can call you James. Are you from around here?"

"I'm a native Seattleite."

James moved closer to Grayce and whispered in her ear, "She might have gone to Afghanistan, but it's obvious she hasn't spent a lot of time on Capitol Hill."

"I'm born and raised in Seattle, Angie. How about you?"

"I'm like you, sir. I grew up in the Rainier Valley."

Mitzi started to yelp and sprinted ahead of them.

"She might have found something." Angie broke into a fast run, her backpack swaying.

"You didn't say anything about running. Since you've been on this homeless kick, I've ruined my pair of Lanvins. And I refuse to run in my Gucci running shoes."

"First of all there is no need to run. But why wouldn't you run in your running shoes?"

"They're Gucci running shoes. Gucci. G-U-C-C-I."

"I know how to spell Gucci."

"They're a fashion statement, not an actual athletic shoe."

Grayce had always told James that he rivaled Kenneth Branagh on his delivery of a dramatic monologue. Of course, Kenneth Branagh was a trained Shakespearean actor versus James who relied on natural talent. And Kenneth Branagh got paid for it. A lot.

Grayce and James descended down a long bend to a clearing where someone definitely had been camping. In the small space under a fir tree, there was a sleeping bag, flashlight and a bag of kitty litter.

Mitzi sniffed around the sleeping bag and the kitty litter and then widened her search to a six-foot perimeter.

Angie walked a few feet ahead, checking in the low scrub.

Grayce stepped closer to the sleeping bag. Apprehension skimmed over her skin and the back of her knees, like the sensation of looking over the edge of a cliff.

"I get a sleeping bag and a flashlight, but what's with kitty litter?" James asked.

Grayce turned around, searching for the source of her sudden uneasiness.

"A finicky cat who refuses to use the outdoors?" James looked over one shoulder with his head tilted. "Honestly, I don't blame the cat. I refuse to go to concerts where you have to use a port-a-potty."

Mitzi yelped at them and hurried down the path.

"Guess that means we're to follow," Angie said.

Angie turned back toward James. "Terrorists use kitty litter to mask the scent from bomb sniffing dogs."

Grayce felt like she had run into an electric fence. The shocking current ran up and down her body.

James put his hands on his waist. "Honey, are you saying we found the sleeping bag of a terrorist?"

"I'm not sure, sir, if we can jump to that conclusion yet."

"I love jumping to the more interesting, illogical conclusion. Why dwell on a finicky cat when you can consider a terrorist? It must get heavy for a terrorist to carry a small bag of kitty litter along with every bomb."

Grayce listened with half an ear to James' newest drama.

Mitzi returned to sniffing the sleeping bag. Whining, she walked around the bag, then delved into the opening and pulled out a sheet of paper.

Grayce bent down to see what Mitzi had recovered. "What did you find, girl?"

James and Angie came over to inspect the discovery.

Grayce scanned the paper. "It's a detailed map of Jack Block Park." Hot and cold chills ran up Grayce's arms.

Grayce showed the paper to James and Angie. "Where is Jack Block Park?"

James said, "It's in West Seattle. It was the site of an old wood treatment plant, then a shipbuilding plant. Contaminated with creosote, it was cleaned up with Superfund money in the 90's."

"How do you know so much about this stuff?" Angie asked James.

"I follow the building changes that happen in the city."

"A terrorist who wants to bomb Jack Block Park? It's very close to the shipyard," Angie said.

"I'm going to put the map back where we found it." Grayce didn't want to handle the map for some reason. She lifted the flap of the sleeping bag and tucked the map back inside. Her hands were shaking." I think we should leave."

"Yeah, let's get outta here." Angie glanced up the hill.

"You don't want to do a stakeout?" James asked.

Angie turned and confronted James. "This is all a joke to you, isn't it?"

"Kind of. I feel like I'm in Hercule Poirot novel."

"Hercule Poirot?" Angie asked.

"James loves Hercule Poirot because he's a very self-involved character who is fastidious about his appearance," Grayce added.

"What does a French novel have to do with my friend?"

"Agatha Christie wasn't French and neither was Poirot. He was Belgian." James said.

"Belgian? What the hell are you talking about? Are you for real? You with the perfect life, the perfect designer clothes. You've got no idea about the heavy shit the rest of us are dealing with."

James dug into the dirt with his Gucci shoe in a very unlike James manner. "Angie, honey, I'm sorry. I'm not making fun of you. I respect that you're willing to come out here after what you've been through in the last few days." James kicked more dirt with his shoe. "I make jokes...it's my way of lightening up reality."

Angie held her clenched fists at her side. "I've had a short fuse since I got back stateside. I'm sorry, sir." Conflicting emotions moved across her face. "Dr. Walters told me about how you and she searched the condemned building for me."

"It was the least Grayce and I could do after what you and Maddy have done for our country. We owe you that and more. I could never serve in Afghanistan..." James ran hands through his hair, teasing the curls into a perfect coiffed style. My hair can't take the sand."

Angie pressed her lips together as if she was ready to laugh. "But the sand does great things for your skin, kind of like getting a daily facial peel."

"Is there a girlfriend under the macho clothes and kick-ass attitude?"

Angie and James shared a real belly laugh. The delightful sound resounded in the woods with the morning songbirds.

The happy noise didn't relieve Grayce of the perception that evil was lurking nearby.

"I don't think Maddy is hiding out here. Let's head back," Angie said.

"Praise the Lord. How about breakfast, ladies? My treat. Columbia City has a great bakery and breakfast joint."

"Wait a minute. Where's Mitzi?" Distracted by the clashes between James and Angie, Grayce had lost track of Mitzi, last seen sniffing in the bushes.

With the mention of her name, Mitzi came bounding up the hillside. Mitzi had been searching, but no bark meant she hadn't been successful in finding clues about Maddy.

Grayce couldn't shake the certainty that they were missing something.

"Okay, Mitzi. Let's go." Angie asserted herself as leader.

Mitzi ran ahead. Her band of explorers followed.

Finding the kitty litter and the map had to be more than a coincidence.

"Do you think we should call the police and report what we've found?" Grayce asked.

"I was wondering the same thing," Angie answered. "I'm not sure what they would do. By the time they get out here, the person will be long gone."

"I read somewhere that the terrorists hide among the homeless. Or maybe it was a plot on one of the TV shows," James added.

"I'm going to take a picture on my phone just in case." Grayce had decided that she would call Davis in DC. He'd know how to proceed with possible terrorist conspiracies.

"Angie, did your brother leave Seattle?" Grayce asked.

"Time out." James bent down. "I've got a rock in my shoe."

Angie turned back. "Hunter's staying around for a while. He said he had business to handle before he left."

"Your mom said he was in the military?" It wasn't the whole truth, but Mrs. Hines had started to tell Grayce about Hunter's background.

"Hunter was a Marine, and both our dads are Marines."

Angie sure didn't chat like most people. "Oh, he's not now?"

"Not sure what he is doing exactly. He doesn't discuss it."

Grayce's suspicions were growing like the wild foxgloves scattered across the hillside.

"You think he's doing something secretive?" Grayce didn't add "or criminal."

"Yeah, I'm thinking FBI or CIA."

Grayce's heart accelerated, thumping against her chest.

"Isn't it amazing that such a tiny little rock can cause such agony?" James held up a little pebble.

"Agony?" Angie guffawed. "Honey, you don't know what agony is." She mimicked James' over-the-top intonation exactly. "Are you ready, Sir James?"

"Watch out, girlfriend, two can play this game." James lifted his perfectly shaped eyebrows and then started up the hill.

Grayce didn't want to end the discussion about Hunter. She followed behind Angie. "It was really nice of your brother to come out and help your mom." This was a real stretch, but Hunter did help find Angie.

"Surprised me that he would help. We've never been close. He had a lot of anger toward my mom when she married his dad."

All the pieces were falling into place, but why had he come to help? And Grayce did believe he was CIA. It fit.

"OMG. This climb is a workout." James panted. It was all an act. James was a gym-rat and totally fit.

Aunt Aideen had predicted that Hunter would bring danger to her and Davis. How would that be possible if he were FBI? But if he were CIA that would be different..

"I'm having a double espresso ASAP."

It was going to be a long drive back to Fremont.

CHAPTER TWENTY-FOUR

Brandon hurried down the steep, narrow path in the *jungle*. He moved his stash every morning to a different spot on the vertical incline, so he was able to avoid all the losers who wandered down the main path in the woods.

He'd become more cautious after a street drunk told him that the police sometimes came with sniffing dogs, but he wasn't sure whether they were looking for bombs or bongs. Brandon hoped the cops weren't searching for ammo, but for drugs or criminals. He assumed the canines weren't trained for bomb sniffing, but he wasn't taking any chances. He had only five days to go and God help him if he fucked up now.

He stopped when he heard voices below him on the main track. He distinctly heard a woman's voice. God, he hoped it wasn't that pimp who brought his women to the isolated area to beat them into submission.

He slowed, careful not to draw attention. They were really close to his hideout. His scalp tingled with the threat.

Hiding behind the trunk of a large tree, he peered down on three people talking.

Red rage exploded behind his eyes like a nuclear blast. It was Grayce Walters, the veterinarian, from the newspaper and the 65th Street house. What the fuck was she doing in the *jungle*? But of course he knew the answer to that. Obviously she had come looking for him.

The same nelly dude was with her, but the tatted woman wasn't. This woman was dressed and stood like a soldier. What the fuck? It was the woman who had been in his house and now she was looking for him, too.

Grayce Walters, the meddling whore, was talking about the police. She turned her head and he missed the rest, but he definitely heard police. Panic raced into each of his nerves and then pummeled his heart.

Throwing caution aside, he left his hiding place and painstakingly made his way down through tree roots and low bushes, trying not to make noise until he loomed twenty feet over them.

The other woman was definitely military. Why were she and Grayce Walters together?

Grayce Walters was going on—just like his mother. Now she asked questions about the hunter.

The guy was nattering about something as he reached into his shoe.

The soldier said FBI and CIA. Fuck. He felt like ants were running up his legs. He couldn't stand still. He fisted his hands around the tree. He wanted to choke the shit out of Grayce Walters, the meddling bitch.

Suddenly the damn poodle ran from the hill below the track.

He stopped breathing and stood frozen. The sound of his heartbeat reverberated in his ears. He waited with his Glock drawn.

Stupid dog didn't look up, but ran up the path with the three people following. They continued their conversation about the hunter as they walked up the trail.

He waited, taking his breaths in fast pants. He wanted to take a deep breath, but was afraid to move, make a sound.

Had they found his belongings? There was nothing to find—only his sleeping bag. He needed to calm down. He was too close to let two snooping bitches interfere.

He had to take care of Grayce Walters. The newspaper made it so easy. She practiced in Fremont. It was time for Gator. He'd stop the bitch, oh, yeah.

CHAPTER TWENTY-FIVE

Grayce sat in the passenger seat of James' red convertible Beamer. With the roof down, she had tied a scarf around her hair so that her hairdo wouldn't end up looking like the Bride of Frankenstein for Duke's, a Doberman pinscher, funeral.

Beyoncé's "Partition"—"*I just want to be the girl you like*" blasted out of the Blaupunkt speaker system. Well, that's what James said it was—Blaupunkt. Or was it Bose?

"I couldn't have faced today without you." James turned down the music. "Have you been to a dog's funeral before?"

Grayce didn't tell James that she hadn't been to a funeral since Cassie's. And really didn't want to remember that day.

"Wimp...that's what my father used to call me and he was right—I am a wimp. I agreed to attend the funeral since I felt guilty for not attending the viewing. OMG, can you imagine seeing a Doberman pinscher laid out in a casket?"

Grayce would've made an understanding comment, but the years of friendship had taught her it was better to let James vent.

"And OMG what kind of relatives have a pet viewing?"

"James, I think you might have gotten it wrong about the viewing.

Pets aren't embalmed. They are cremated.

""Really? Oh, thank God. Maybe my relatives aren't as nuts as I thought."

"I've never heard you talk about these relatives," Grayce said.

"My father didn't exactly get along with his own side of the family. And he definitely didn't want to parade his gay son in front of them."

Grayce tried hard not to criticize James' father, but there were times when it was really difficult.

"When my aunt's husband died, my Uncle Foster, the bigtime personal injury attorney died. I knew my dad wouldn't attend. Foster was better than him at everything. Golf. Cards. Tennis. Drinking... my father never gave up trying to beat him at that last one though."

Grayce nodded.

"My Aunt Pat can't possibly be related to my dad. She's soft, kind, and loving. And I liked my cousin right away. My aunt talked to me about my mom—how much she missed her."

Grayce reached over and squeezed James' arm. "How wonderful to talk about your mom."

"I planned to take my aunt to lunch, then Kip's dog died unexpectedly and he called me. I wasn't sure if I could face the entire family. I don't want to be the center of family gossip."

"Am I hearing this right?" Grayce placed her hand on heart. "You don't want to be the center of attention? My heart is going into arrhythmia."

"Very funny, and for that comment, I'm going to make sure your scarf comes off."

James accelerated down Highway 99.

They both laughed when the wind blew Grayce's scarf off, but she grabbed the piece of silk before it sailed down the freeway.

James slowed for the exit. "Remember in *Bridget Jones* when she pretends to be Grace Kelly in *To Catch a Thief?* Instead of the perfect, sophisticated Grace Kelly, Bridget's scarf flies off, ruining her hair."

James leaned over and fluffed her bangs at the stop sign. "Your thick hair still looks great, even wind tousled. "Did Davis get to see you this morning in your little black dress from Helene and your sexy Louboutins?"

"He didn't. He left for DC before I got ready."

"Why don't you do a selfie, right now? You look fabulous."

"What a great idea." She and Davis needed to lighten up, have some fun, since their time together had gotten stilted with their separation.

She dug in her black Prada purse, a present from her mom, for her phone. She took a picture of James driving in his Ray Ban sunglasses. And then one of herself. She texted Davis-"summer in Seattle."

They drove down a hill into a park-like field dotted with head-stones and memorials. "Why did we come?" James' face took on a deathly color.

He looked around the cemetery and exhaled a deep breath. "Thanks for coming, darling, I know it isn't what you wanted to do, but I couldn't face a dog's funeral without you."

James pulled his car into the line of cars at the mortuary. A chunky man with the same dark, curly hair as James, waved a hand-kerchief at them to join the line of cars. James' Beamer was the seventh car in line behind the ominous, black hearse.

"I didn't expect so many people," Grayce said.

James looked askance at her, over the rims of his Ray Bans, "You and your children will have to drive separately so I can have at least as many cars as Duke."

"My children? What are you talking about?"

"Honey, I know you're the queen of predictions, but I'm the queen of everything else. And I predict that I'm going to be an Uncle Jamesie many times over."

Grayce couldn't enjoy the teasing, since her fear around the sepa-ration from Davis was rearing its head. James would see all her issues right out front.

James and Grayce followed the line of cars and parked at the gravesite.

"God, I can't believe we're doing this." James checked his tie before he opened the door.

His cousin was walking down the aisle of cars, greeting everyone.

James came around to open Grayce's door as his cousin walked up to them.

"Cuz, I'm glad you could get away from work." Kip hugged James in bear hug. "Thank you for coming." Kip was a burly guy with what her mother would have described as apple cheeks. In his black suit with his blonde crew-cut, he looked a little bit like Goldfinger.

"Kip, this is my good friend, Grayce Walters." She had asked James not to share her profession since she wanted to be a guest only.

"Thank you for bringing him." Kip looked at Grayce, but stuck his thumb in James' direction. "I know he didn't want to come."

James didn't say anything. He adjusted his sunglasses on his face.

Kip handed Grayce a single, red rose from a bouquet he held and a program with a picture of a gigantic Doberman who was full of life and smiling. "The program is in honor ..." his words faltered.

Grayce took the rose from Kip's hand and took his hand in hers, sending him all her comfort. "I'm sorry for your loss. Duke looks like a very happy dog in the picture. He was well-loved."

Kip rubbed his eyes with the backs of his stubby hands and cleared his throat. "Will you escort Aunt Sonja to the gravesite, James? She's two cars ahead."

James took Grayce's arm since she would have trouble walking on the uneven grass in her Louboutins.

James opened his aunt's car door. "Aunt Sonja, I'm to be your escort." He bowed formally as if in an English ballroom to the small, round lady.

"You sweet boy. Come and give me a kiss."

James leaned into the car, giving the woman a brief peck before helping his aunt step out..

Aunt Sonja had brown, rheumy eyes with a mischievous light.

"Brought yourself a beautiful beard?" Aunt Sonja inspected Grayce from her Louboutins to Helene's dress and little black sweater.

James and Grayce laughed together.

"How do you know about beards?" James asked.

"You gotta keep up if you want to be an interesting old lady."

"Aunt Sonja, this is my dear friend, Grayce Walters."

"Give me your arm, young lady. You're going to need my help to walk in those high heels."

Grayce wanted to laugh aloud again but restrained herself. She knew exactly where James got his chutzpah.

"You don't need to pretend you're something you're not in order to be with family, James."

"Then you don't know my father very well."

"Of course I know your father. He's my brother. Men can be so silly. Poor Bertie, he could never do right in our father's eyes."

"Poor Bertie? You've got to be kidding?" James' voice had taken on an edge.

"Your father treated you exactly how he was treated. I'm sorry, but you've got to forgive your father. Anger will eat you up."

Kip walked up to their group, interrupting the tense moment. "Aunt Sonja, I've a chair for you."

People walked toward the casket resting in a deep hole in the ground. "Amazing Grace" played from a CD player on a table with a white tablecloth and a bouquet of red roses. The quiet talking stopped at the sight of the casket.

Kip stood near the grave and signaled for the music to be turned down. He dabbed at his eyes with a white handkerchief. "Your presence helps my loss..." His voice quavered and he cleared his throat. "I've asked my sister Dorothy to do a reading you'll find printed in your program."

Dorothy, a lean woman with metal gray hair, walked and stood next to Kip. Her hand shook as she read in a quiet voice, "Friend, please don't mourn for me, I'm still here, though you don't see. I'm right by your side each night and day and within your heart I long to stay. My body is gone but I'm always near. I'm everything you feel, see or hear. My spirit is free, but I'll never depart as long as you keep me alive in your heart. I'll never wander out of your sight—I'm the brightest star on a summer night."

The words of loss hit Grayce. Tears welled in her eyes. She dug in her purse for a Kleenex as the tears dripped down her face. She cried for the memory of the young girl who lost her sister and best friend and the many beloved pets she helped cross the rainbow.

Aunt Sonja wept into her handkerchief, too. Grayce understood that this funeral must be very difficult for James' aunt after the recent loss of her husband. She felt like a sham, being upset that she and Davis would be separated for six months, watching the older woman grieve.

James hid behind his Ray Ban sunglasses, but Grayce didn't believe he was unaffected by the grief.

A short man with a balding head and glasses spoke next. "Can you join hands as we recite St. Francis' prayer? St. Francis was the gentle patron saint of animals."

Grayce took James' hand. James voice was steady as he recited the prayer and Grayce wondered if his aunt's advice had affected him during the part of prayer—*in forgiving there is forgiveness.*

Kip tossed his rose on the top of the casket. His sister Dorothy was next, followed by Aunt Sonja. Everyone tossed their roses on the shiny wood casket, making a glorious bed of flowers out of grief and loss. Celine Dion's haunting song "Because You Loved Me" played.

The bald man spoke, breaking the painful sobs in the quiet. "Kip would like all of you to join him at Ray's Boathouse after the service. A light luncheon will be served."

James cursed under his breath. "I can't do this. Let's go."

Grayce took his arm. "Don't you want to say good-bye?"

James shook his head and started to walk toward the car. "I'll call them next week."

CHAPTER TWENTY-SIX

Grayce came out of the veterinarian clinic and walked down Upper Queen Anne Avenue, glad to have finished the acupuncture demonstration—her second this week. She found it challenging to limit her teaching to the clinical aspect of acupuncture and not the art of energy healing. Treating energy was a personal and spiritual journey that a practitioner had to embrace.

Exhausted from the sleepless nights, she needed caffeine before heading back to the stacked charts on her desk. There were coffee shops on every block on both upper and lower Queen Anne. The day had clouded over. There was an eminent feeling of sudden rain with the dark sky hovering overhead.

Grayce buttoned her sweater against the quickening cool breeze. An anxious dog yelped behind her. She turned to the distressed animal's sound.

A Cattle Dog squealed in excitement as his owner came out of the grocery store. A tall, dark man walking behind her suddenly turned and bent over the newspaper. The man looked like Hunter Hines. He was dressed in the same blue shirt and pants that Hunter always wore.

Grayce's stomach churned in apprehension. She turned and walked a few steps to peer into the next shop window. She feigned interest in hair salon products as she watched the man through the window's reflection. He remained bent over with his head turned away, as if he knew she watched him. He stood and walked in the other direction.

He resembled Hunter Hines in both size and coloring. The only difference was this man slouched. It couldn't be Hunter Hines, could it? Why would Hunter Hines be following her? The memory of Aunt Aideen's prediction caused anxious dread to move through her.

Lost in thought, she had been standing in front of the window for several minutes. She looked back into the window to make sure Hunter Hines was gone and caught the reflection of a young guy in a gray hoodie, leaning over a car. His face was angled down away from her, but he had multiple facial piercings like the kid Gator at Teen Feed.

She was losing it. Without sleep and without Davis, she was imagining men following her on Queen Anne. If she didn't get some sleep soon, she was going to become as dramatic as James.

She decided to skip the tea and head to her office. The sooner she got the work done, the sooner she could go home. She wanted to go to bed and sleep through the night without dreaming, not awaken alone in the dark.

Mitzi waited for her in the car. The poodle had caused such a scene howling and hurdling herself at the door with Grayce's departure that Grayce had relented and brought Mitzi. It seemed she wasn't the only one who was having trouble adjusting to Davis' absence. And he was gone for only ten days. What was it going to be like for her and Mitzi after he'd been gone for six months?

Grayce walked toward her car. She turned back to see if the Gator look-alike was still at the car, but he was gone. She couldn't shake the sensation of approaching danger. And then it struck her, it was the same perception that she had felt at the house on 65th Street. She was becoming paranoid.

Instead of her usual exuberant greeting, Mitzi was agitated, barking forcefully when Grayce got to the car. She unlocked the car.

"What's the matter, Mitzi? Do you need to go for a walk?"

Grayce reached in the back seat for the leash. Mitzi howled. "I was only gone for two hours and you wanted to come, remember?"

Mitzi jumped out of the car, but instead of waiting for her leash, she ran circles around the car, growling insistently.

"What is the matter?"

People were staring as Mitzi circled the car for the third time. Exhausted, Grayce had little patience for the dog's erratic behavior.

"Mitzi, it's okay. I'll take you for a long walk along the canal when we get back to my office. Okay?"

Mitzi paced around the car and snarled. Was Mitzi trying to warn her? Suddenly Grayce felt her senses overwhelmed, as if her nerve ending were exploding.

"Okay, girl. I get it. Let's go."

Grayce searched down the street. She had the same sensation of a malevolent presence as when she had walked in the *jungle* on Beacon Hill.

Grayce pointed to the passenger door. Mitzi didn't do her usual leap into the car, but whimpered when she took her place next to Grayce on the passenger side.

Grayce turned around, looking one last time behind her before she got in her car. She was spooked. First Hunter, then Gator and now Mitzi's agitation. She exhaled deeply and got in the Outback.

She drove north on Queen Anne, debating if she should follow her expected pattern of returning to her office or drive to James' office. She'd head to her office to decide whether she was being followed, and if so, then she'd drive to James' downtown office. She didn't want to be trapped alone in her upstairs office... Like last time.

Grayce checked her rear view mirror frequently to see if anyone followed her. She had only seen in the movies where people could tell they were being followed and wasn't sure how she'd know. A silver-haired woman in a SUV drove behind her.

The large vehicle prevented Grayce from seeing the cars behind her.

Mitzi kept a low keening whimper.

"I'm sorry. I didn't mean to be cross with you. You were trying to warn me. Someone is following us."

Mitzi turned and looked to the side and behind her. The dog's instincts were on high alert.

Grayce drove to the intersection of McGraw and Third Street. She might be able see around the SUV at the four-way stop.

There was little resistance on the brake pedal when she hit the brake. She noted the change, but was focused on whether Gator or Hunter followed her.

She made the right turn down the north side of Queen Anne hill. The hill was a half mile long and ended at busy Nickerson Street. After a few blocks, she'd be in Fremont and then at her office.

Mitzi started a low snarl when Grayce turned the corner. The unnerving sound hit Grayce straight in the back of her neck at the top of her spine.

"What is it Mitzi? Did you see someone? Gator?" Grayce checked her rear view mirror again. Nothing.

She braked as she started the sharp descent. Her brakes didn't respond. The car didn't slow. Her foot went to the floor as she pushed on the pedal, but nothing happened. She pumped the brakes. Shit, she didn't remember if she was supposed to pump or not. The car was gaining momentum. There was a minivan in front of her, and if she didn't slow down, she and Mitzi would ram the car.

Grayce frantically pumped the brakes again. Nothing happened. Her heart raced as did the car.

Her brakes were failing on one of Seattle's longest and steepest hills.

Details came into sharp focus as the adrenaline pumped through her. She could see a blond head in a car seat in the back of the van. She'd have to pass the car ahead of her on the congested two way street.

She swerved into the other lane and passed the slow minivan.

She missed the oncoming Volvo by a mere five feet. The Volvo driver honked and screamed at her.

Her hands shook. Sweat was pooling under her arms.

She slowly pulled on the parking brake. It took all her self-control not to jerk the parking brake hard. She remembered something about the back wheels locking if she pulled too fast.

The hand brake didn't slow them as they gained momentum on the vertical incline. She pulled on the parking break again then shifted down into second gear. The car jerked, sending Mitzi forward off the seat. The smell of the burning brake filled the car.

The Subaru careened downhill. Residential houses whizzed by. Fortunately there wasn't another car in front of her for a hundred feet. She'd soon be at the campus of SPU, the scene of a school shooting. They definitely didn't need another tragedy.

They were going too fast for her and Mitzi to jump out of the car, but she couldn't let them rocket into the heavy thoroughfare of Nickerson Street. She had to find a place to slow the car down before she hurt someone.

Fifty feet ahead was a crosswalk filled with students from the college campus. She didn't have anywhere to slow the car without crashing into a tree or building. Her options flashed fast. She could hit the curb, but at this speed, there was a chance of losing control and hitting an oncoming car.

She pulled again on the hand brake and shifted to first simultaneously. The car jerked violently, but this time Mitzi remained seated.

"Mitzi get in the back seat and lie down."

Mitzi's ears went up at the sharp command, but the poodle didn't budge from her seat. She defied Grayce for the first time ever.

Shifting into first had slowed the car so that she was going approximately the same speed as the Lexus in front of her. She could possibly make it to the small park on the corner near Nickerson. She could use the evergreen shrubs to stop the car. And hopefully not hit any pedestrians on the way.

She pumped the brake again to see if there was any friction. Nothing.

"Oh, no."

The Lexus in front of her had put on the left-hand signal. The traffic heading up the hill was bumper to bumper. The Lexus and she would need to stop. Her heart beat frantically.

She pulled on the hand brake. At forty miles an hour, she was going to have to drive up on the right-side curb. The Lexus stopped in front of her. She swerved to avoid smashing the Lexus and then hit the curb.

Grayce veered sharply to the left, missing the Lexus by mere inches. Grayce overcorrected and tried to ride against the curb. She was approaching the crosswalk filled with pedestrians. She had to make a choice in the next fifteen seconds—hit the trees along the curb to stop the car or hurtle into the congested traffic or the college students.

Some observant student had cried out a warning, the crosswalk had cleared and Grayce and Mitzi sailed through.

Grayce sent up a prayer of gratitude, regardless of the irate shouts and fearful screams behind her. Having survived one disaster, Grayce looked at busy Nickerson Street looming.

By some miracle, there were no cars waiting at the light ahead. Grayce now prayed that the light would change so she and Mitzi could turn into the park. And she prayed that there were no people walking on the sidewalk.

The light changed as Grayce and Mitzi came to the intersection and made the right turn to the park. The car's wheels squealed as they took the turn, and the driver's side lifted off the pavement. Grayce took a deep breath and aimed the car at the curb and a clump of small, beautifully pruned and shaped dwarf holly bushes.

She consciously tried to relax. The car hit the curb and Grayce lost control as it careened to the right and slammed into a small tree.

Grayce absorbed the impact in slow motion. Her neck and spine rolled forward and then backward before her head slammed into the steering wheel. . Her last thought was to ask the universe for one last favor—tolet Mitzi be safe.

CHAPTER TWENTY-SEVEN

Grayce heard her name in the distance. The sound was distorted, as if she were swimming underwater. Sirens roared around her. "Dr. Walters. Dr. Walters. Can you open your eyes?"

She didn't want to open her eyes. It would hurt too much. She drifted back into the darkness.

The voice was relentless. She wanted to sleep. She was so tired.

"I'm a friend of Davis'."

Davis. He was going to go ballistic when he heard about the crash.

A cool tongue licked her hand. Grayce opened her eyes. "Mitzi?" A sharp pain cut between her eyes. A sea of blue shirts surrounded her. She recognized the fire department uniform.

A blond man kneeling next to her held her hand. "I'm Davis' climbing buddy, Chris Crosby. You've had a car accident."

"No accident." Her voice came out raspy as if she had gone without water.

"Is Mitzi hurt?" She turned her head to look at the poodle, but the small movement blasted violent pain into her head, as if her head might explode.

"Except for a few bruises and cuts she got with the impact, Mitzi is fine. But you hit your head on the steering wheel and the windshield."

She had a vague memory of hurdling through space before everything went black. "Yes, when my car hit the tree."

"We're going to transport you to Harborview. You're going to need to be checked out. Do you want me to call Davis, have him meet you at the hospital?"

Grayce couldn't concentrate because of the pain, but she knew she didn't want to alarm Davis. There was nothing he could do three thousand miles away. "Davis is out of town. I'll call my friend James to pick me up once they run the tests. I'm sure I'm fine."

"But Davis will want to know. He won't be happy that we treated you and then didn't call him."

"Chris, please don't call Davis." She touched Chris' hand. "He can't do anything in DC, and the call will only upset him. I'll call him once I'm checked out, okay? But can you take Mitzi with you until someone can pick her up?"

"Don't worry about Mitzi. I'll take care of her, but Davis is going to be rip roaring mad if I don't call him."

"He won't be. I promise to tell him you wanted to call, okay?"

Chris rubbed his chin. "What did you mean earlier when you said that this crash wasn't an accident?"

"My brakes were tampered with. They failed coming down Third Street. I had to hit the tree to avoid injuring anyone."

"How do you know your brakes were tampered with?"

"Two men were following me, and the brake failure is too much of a coincidence."

"Crosby, that's enough, man." Another blue uniform put his hand on Chris' arm. "I need to get her to Harborview. The police can talk to her later."

Grayce closed her eyes, trying to use meditation to block the overwhelming pain that consumed her. The firefighters' conversation came in and out of her consciousness.

Chris was talking about Davis and how he'd want all the details.

But the other blue uniform was telling Chris that she might be confused from the accident and not to alarm Davis. Davis and he could get all the information from the police.

She wanted to correct the medic's wrong conclusion, but she couldn't summon the energy to argue. She was convinced that either Hunter Hines or Gator had messed with her brakes as Aunt Aideen had predicted. But the medics would definitely think she had a serious brain injury if she mentioned the tarot card reading.

CHAPTER TWENTY-EIGHT

Davis couldn't breathe. Every time he thought of Grayce careening down Third Avenue, his chest tightened, refusing to move air. He'd been in some sticky situations on mountain climbs, and overcome the deadly reaction. But when it came to Grayce, he couldn't control the panic that made him breathless, air hungry.

He drove well over the speed limit on 99 to get to Grayce's house. He had hoped to arrive in time to be with Grayce in the hospital, but the red-eye flight had been delayed. She'd been discharged.

Without James' phone call, he wouldn't have known about Grayce's accident or hospitalization. Grayce was doing it again. Keeping secrets to protect him. He could already hear her reasoning that she hadn't wanted him to worry, leave his new position.

Twenty minutes max and he'd be at Grayce's house. He'd texted James for updates. Grayce had been diagnosed with a mild concussion. Her CAT scan had been clear. She had two shiners and looked like she had come out of a boxing match.

Thank God James had his back and was texting him with

updates. Grayce hadn't told her parents or him about her little accident.

He looked down at the stuffed bear he'd picked up during his layover in Chicago. There were no flowers at O'Hare.

CHAPTER TWENTY-NINE

Wrapped in a down duvet, Grayce sat on the couch with Napoleon, her Maine Coon cat, settled in the folds. Her head throbbed, her eyes burned and she had the headache from hell. She should place a few acupuncture needles, but she was too exhausted to care. She couldn't get warm even though the day was sunny and mild—likely delayed shock from the accident.

"Now that you're home you have to call your parents and Davis." James sat across from her. He didn't look his usual, perfectly coiffed self. His hair was unkempt; his pressed shirt and pants were wrinkled. He had been with her in the ER during the entire 10-hour ordeal. Because of her brief loss of consciousness, she had to stay in the observation unit for eight hours.

A depressing lethargy had enveloped her since she got home. She couldn't face her parents or Davis' worries. She just wanted to sink into a sleeping oblivion like Napoleon.

"Do you have any idea what the news of my car accident is going to do to my parents?" She found her chest tightening. "Tear them apart."

James reached over and patted her hand. "You need to call them and tell them you're not seriously injured. Imagine if they saw the news that you had been in an accident."

"My parents never watch TV. They haven't seen it, or they would've called. My accident will dredge up all their memories of Cassie's accident."

"They're your parents. Let them take care of you. You don't need to shield them any longer."

She really didn't want to dissect her traumatic adolescence when her head felt as if screws had been drilled into her forehead. More than anything, she wanted to go to bed and delay dealing with everyone's emotions until tomorrow.

"James, don't say anything else. I know I need to call my parents and Davis, but I'm too tired and overwhelmed to present the accident in a way that won't upset them. When Davis finds out, he'll want to leave his new job and fly here immediately. And when he finds out that the brakes were sabotaged, he'll never leave Seattle again. I don't want him to give up this opportunity. I have to downplay the whole episode to keep him in DC and right now I don't have the strength. My head feels as if it's caught in a vise, and every time I move the vise tightens."

"You've been hurt. You need to let the people who love you take care of you."

"You're right, but can you imagine my parent's reaction if they see the bruises and black eyes?" She gently touched the five inch contusion on her forehead. "I don't want to think about Davis' reaction if he saw me right now." She shuddered.

"I'm sure Davis loves raccoons."

"That's supportive."

"Of course they're going to be upset to see you hurt, but more so if you don't notify them. You don't have to handle everything alone anymore. You've got Davis."

"I want to tell Davis when Mitzi's with me."

"You're stalling, Grayce. Davis will not be worried about Mitzi's whereabouts. She's with one of his best friends. And about Davis..." James gave a tiny cough behind his hand. "There is something I've been waiting to tell you until you were safe at home."

James stood and walked to the window at the sound of a car pulling into the driveway.

She heard keys jangling. There was only one person beside James who had a key to her house.

"Davis knows?" Her heart tattooed an irregular rhythm against her chest.

James nodded. "I was about to tell you."

"You called him?" She was incredulous.

"When you were having your CAT scan."

In the ten seconds it took Davis to open the door, every emotion went through her in a flash. She hadn't washed her face or combed her hair, and she wore her ratty jammies. She didn't want Davis to see her injuries. She didn't want to upset him. She needed rest before she could present a cheerful and normal facade when he walked through the door.

"Grayce." His voice was ragged with emotion. He crossed the room in his powerful strides and stood in front of her.

When she saw the torment in his eyes, she knew that she had made the biggest mistake of her life. The hurt that flashed in his usually bright eyes did something terrible to her stomach.

James tried to ease the dreadful tension. "You made it back to Seattle in record time, Davis."

Grayce saw the lines of exhaustion under Davis' eyes, his crumpled clothes, and grasped in his hand, a brown teddy bear wearing a Cubs jersey, and a red, velvet bow tied around its neck. His raw, disheveled masculine appearance and the teddy bear melted all her defenses.

Davis didn't answer James.

"Now that you're here, my job is done. Grayce has been impossible since the accident, screaming for more narcotics and whining about the long wait in the ER. Oh wait, that wasn't Grayce, that was me."

James walked over to the sofa and gave Grayce a kiss, European style, on both cheeks. "Au revoir. Thank you for a very interesting night at Harborview. Tsk, tsk. Almost as entertaining as the night I planned dancing at Neighbors Nightclub." James leaned over and whispered close to her ear. "Honey, you're in trouble. Tarzan looks like he's going to go all primitive."

Davis shook James' hand. "Thank you for everything. I appreciated your texts keeping me apprised."

Guilt washed over Grayce in tidal wave proportions.

James turned away from Davis and gave her the sign of having her throat slit.

Davis hadn't moved from the middle of the room. He stared at her as if to reassure himself that she was real. She stood and threw herself into his arms. She hadn't realized how much she needed his steady presence, his warmth around her. Davis tossed the teddy bear on a chair and wrapped her in his strong arms.

He held her tight against his chest. She could hear his steady heartbeat. They stood together savoring the moment.

She didn't want to ruin their closeness, but she had to apologize. She should have called him. "You're upset."

"Upset?" He dropped his arms. "Of course, I'm upset. Upset that you were in an accident, upset that you didn't call me."

Grayce suddenly felt cold and bereft without the warmth and security of Davis' arms. She had hurt him. She hadn't meant to.

Davis walked toward the windows and stood with his back to her. "I wanted to share the worst with you, be by your side, take care of you." He shook his body as if getting rid of all his pent up emotions. "You would've called me tomorrow and pretended that you hadn't suffered."

"I made a mistake, but it was in the best way of believing I was protecting you. I'm really sorry."

He turned and stared at her. His words were clipped. "You weren't protecting me. You were protecting yourself. You wanted to decide when and how you would deal with me. I don't want to be dealt with."

She had the overpowering sensation of falling in all directions at once. "If you were in Seattle, I would've called you. Don't you understand, but you were 3000 miles away. What could you have done?" Shaky, she sat back down on the couch.

"What I did—get on a plane, call the hospital, call the police. And if I had met your parents, I could've called them. But you don't want that, do you Grayce? You're not ready for me to really be part of your life."

"This is so unfair. And what do my parents have to do with this conversation?"

He walked toward her, his hands fisted at his sides. "You've made a commitment to me. Or I thought you had, but I've never met your parents? Why is that?"

"Davis, I can't believe you're bringing this up now?"

"You told me I was trying to put our relationship on a time table, but that's exactly what you've done. When will be the right time for you to admit you need me? One year? Two years?"

The room started to spin and Grayce didn't know if it was from Davis' words or the look on his pained face.

"Davis, I can't have this conversation right now." She was too tired to make sense of what was happening.

He stood over her and looked at her, from the swollen, red contusion on her forehead to the purple and blue shiners under her eyes. "My God. You could've been killed." She heard the fear in his voice.

"I'm okay, just some bruises, but I'm tired from my night in the hospital."

She knew by the way Davis' neck and shoulders tightened that she had made a mistake by reminding him of her hospitalization. His eyes clouded with an emotion she couldn't decipher.

He walked toward the door and then turned back, his hand on

the door knob. His voice was even and flat, always a sign that he was struggling with his feelings. "You need to rest. I've got to check in with the chief since I left DC unexpectedly. I'll call you later."

He walked out and carefully closed the door. His considerate behavior was worse than if he had slammed the door.

CHAPTER THIRTY

D avis got into his car and drove away from Grayce and the pain. He couldn't shake the image of Grayce, dazed and pale.

Didn't she understand? She could've been killed. When he looked at her, really looked, and saw the bruises and swelling, he wanted to take her in his arms and hold her and never let her suffer. But she had rejected his support. When she had been at her lowest, she didn't allow herself to call him, need him.

His anger and worry were all jumbled together. He couldn't stand the confusing torment. He had to take a break, get away from the claustrophobic feeling.

He exited I-5 at James Street. He'd stop by the station to let the chief know he was back and then get an update from Chris on the details of the investigation into Grayce's brake failure. He didn't believe that there had been foul play. This was an old Subaru, and Grayce never paid attention to maintenance.

He parked in front of the Pioneer Square Station.

"Shit." Maclean, the assistant chief from hell, was walking right toward him. He didn't have time to hide from the antagonistic jerk.

One of the upsides of the DC position was that he wouldn't see his acerbic supervisor. Former supervisor... now that had a nice ring to it.

"Missing us already?" Maclean's grin was broad and showed his white teeth. And Davis didn't believe the AC's fake bullshit for a second.

"Maclean." Davis wasn't going to get let the jackass get under his skin today.

"Must be the very charming Dr. Walters you were missing." Maclean poked and prodded until he hit his victim's vulnerable spot. "When's the wedding?"

"Don't you ever get tired of being an asshole?" Davis walked away.

He heard Maclean's laughter and mocking voice. "Trouble in paradise, Davis?"

Davis took the steps to the second floor and walked into the chief's office. Sarah, the assistant, was on the phone. She shook her head when Davis pointed to the chief's office.

He walked out of the administrative offices to the station next door. Chris, Steve, and Mike were washing the rig.

"Hey, man, what are you doing here?" Chris held a sponge in the air.

Davis nodded to the guys, but his suppressed angst must have been evident since neither approached him.

He turned his back to the guys and spoke to Chris. "I came to see the chief and hear what you've gotten from the police."

"But you just left for DC."

"Yeah, well, I'm back."

"You want to talk about it?"

"You been watching Dr. Phil? Hell, no, I don't want to talk about it."

Chris shrugged his shoulders. "Okay, man."

Chris dropped his sponge into the bucket. "Hey, guys, can you take over?"

That the guys didn't rib Chris for abandoning them was definitely not a good sign. Over their shoulders, they kept giving Davis furtive looks, watching to see if he might go postal. He took a deep breath. He thought he was in control, but maybe not.

"Listen, man. I'm not sure what's going through your stubborn, mulish, Scottish head, but Grayce is an amazing woman and you shouldn't let her go."

"I'm not letting her go. I'm back to take care of her." His voice cracked in feeling.

Chris put his arm around Davis' shoulder. "I just got off the phone with your best friend in the police department, very special detective, Blake Calfell."

"My best friend? Very funny. Did the bastard give you any information? He pulled the confidentiality shit with me."

"He's enjoying making you squirm, since you made him look bad by solving his case."

"We're supposed to be 'colleagues working in a collaborative relationship' with the police department in solving crimes." Davis quoted the department's bureaucratic jargon. It made no difference to the ongoing territorial pissing games between the detectives and fire investigators.

"Did he tell you anything?" Davis asked.

"The brakes were definitely tampered with. Someone cut the brake line."

Davis exploded in shock and outrage. "Not an accident?" He could barely get the words out. "What else did that bastard say? I can't believe he wouldn't tell me. That bastard."

"Calfell didn't know when he talked to you. He just found out. He's about to call Grayce to interview her. He knew she had been in observation at Harborview."

"I don't want that bastard near Grayce."

"He's really interested in the two men following her."

"Two men? Why am I just hearing this?"

"You're hearing it now. And this isn't your case."

"Hell, if it isn't."

"Calfell called the chief and said you were interfering with police business. The chief told me that this case is off-limits to you. No contact with Calfell."

"You've got to be kidding. That son-of-a-bitch reported me because I called him?"

"I'm telling you he's gunning for you after you got all the attention for solving his case."

"Who were the two men following Grayce?"

"I don't know. The medic wouldn't let me continue questioning her."

In his worry, he hadn't considered the possibility that the brake failure hadn't been an accident. He had to get back to Grayce. He had to protect her.

"Davis, you've got the same look as you do when you're about to take a dumb-ass risk on the mountain. What's going on in your head?"

"I've got to get back to Grayce. They might come after her again." His heart pumped hard, as if he were dangling over a crevasse.

Chris nodded. "For one little woman, Grayce sure gets herself into a lot of trouble."

"Not anymore."

Chris guffawed. "Now you're talking like the Davis I know. Remember, I'm going to be the best man at your wedding."

"Right." He wasn't going to tell Chris that he had just acted like a jackass, and Grayce might not forgive him. His hurt pride didn't matter. He wasn't leaving her until he knew she was safe.

"Where's Mitzi? We need to head over to Grayce's." The tightness in his chest was beginning to ease. He could almost take a breath. He was better at making a plan of action than navigating the mire of his emotions.

"Mitzi's at my place. It'll be good to have Mitzi stay with Grayce."

"I'll be staying with Grayce, too, and Mitzi can go to work with Grayce once she's recovered."

"I swear that poodle understands everything I say. When I told her I'd take her back to Grayce, she settled right down."

"Mitzi is totally attached to Grayce." Since the first time he and Mitzi met Grayce, they had become her devotees.

"You're not kidding. The dog howled like a banshee when they took Grayce in the ambulance. It was pitiful."

He didn't want to relive the images of the accident scene again. He'd played and replayed them since James had called him. The image of Mitzi howling and Grayce being sped to Harborview tore away all his steadfast control. He was going to nail the bastards who hurt Grayce.

He might not be the man she called for help, but he was the one to protect her. He had failed. But he wouldn't fail again.

CHAPTER THIRTY-ONE

Grayce was trapped in a watery grave. Escape was impossible. Her legs and arms wouldn't move. Paralyzed, she was pulled down into the deep, bottomless void. The murky, green water surrounded her. The sound of her rapid breathing echoed in the silent water.

Icy water compressed her chest, suffocating her. She was trapped, alone with no one to help. Her breathing became frantic. She was enveloped in endless fear. She fought the heavy sensation of falling into the emptiness.

Grayce awoke in a dark room. For a few seconds, she couldn't sort out where she was. Then she heard Napoleon's gentle snuffle. Relieved to be awakening in her own bed, she rolled to look at the clock.

With the quick movement, a sharp pain shot through her head, a nasty reminder of her injury. The memory of her car accident and her fight with Davis came rushing back. No surprise that she had nightmares. At least she was spared from dreams of Hunter Hines or Gator.

The clock flashed one AM. After Davis had stormed out of the house, exhausted and discouraged, she had immediately gone to bed. She'd slept ten hours.

She gingerly sat up. Her headache had improved from excruciating to moderate throbbing. She needed a Diet Coke. She doubted she'd find potato chips in the cupboard. She hadn't anticipated that she would have a need for the greasy, salty manna. She certainly wouldn't have anticipated that someone would try to murder her.

Napoleon didn't stir. She delayed bending over to search for her flip-flops for fear of the headache from hell returning. She placed her feet on the floor and bumped against a big, furry mass. Mitzi slept next to her bed.

"Mitzi?" The poodle sat up and nuzzled Grayce's hand with her cold nose. "How's my girl?"

Grayce ran her hand over the dog's chest, feeling for the swelling and bruising the poodle must have sustained in the crash.

"Everything check's out fine...but how did you get in here?"

Had Davis brought the dog and left? With that depressing thought, Grayce stood and walked to the kitchen with Mitzi trailing close behind.

She stopped suddenly when she spotted Davis—his dark head hung over one end of the couch, his feet stuck out the other, and his large body draped over the side.

Grayce wanted to touch him, to soothe away the bad feelings between them. She had tried to take care of him, and he refused to understand.

She watched him sleep—his large chest moving slowly, his spiky lashes spread across his rugged cheekbones. Davis suddenly opened his eyes as if he sensed he was being observed.

"Davis?" Embarrassed to be caught staring at him like a star struck teenager, her tone came out strident. "Why are you sleeping on the couch?"

He rolled off the couch and stood.

The silence grew awkward.

He was still in his rumpled blue shirt and khaki pants. His thick, bristly hair stood up on end.

"I'm not leaving you alone until the bastards are caught."

He came back because he believed she needed help? Not to make up after their fight?

"I know everything. Your brakes were cut, and you believe two guys were trailing you."

"You don't need to do this. The police are on the case."

The flash in his eyes was either anger or pain. He spoke in a calm voice—unnatural and not convincing. "Someone tried to kill you. Do you understand? You need me."

His male, take-charge attitude wasn't what she wanted. She did need him but not as a watchdog. She needed him because she loved him. "If I need protection, I'll hire Nick to protect me. He's a soldier and has special training."

"I'm not leaving. I'm not allowing anything to happen to you." For a brief moment she saw his vulnerability, but it was quickly replaced with coolness.

She had never realized before how much indifference could hurt.

CHAPTER THIRTY-TWO

A fter walking the perimeter, Davis and Mitzi waited for Grayce in his car parked in front of Dr. Z's little Ravenna house. The back garden was enclosed, making entry difficult.

Grace hadn't objected when he said he'd wait for her in the car. She had left him with Mitzi.

For the three days since her car accident, he had guarded her 24/7. He never expected to feel such responsibility for any woman. He wasn't going to let anyone hurt Grayce.

His only break was after her he walked her to the office where Nick took over. He continued to search for Gator without alerting Calfell. Davis was frustrated that he had made no progress mainly because Calfell was blocking all of his inquires. Something or someone was going to have to break soon.

How had his life gotten so out of control? He, of all men, who managed his life sensibly and efficiently, had been taken down by one tiny blond woman with fiery green eyes.

Since the accident, he and Grayce had remained in a holding pattern, maintaining a wary distance. It seemed that they were both afraid to discuss their feelings. Maybe it meant Grayce still cared and didn't want to risk ruining their future. That thought gave him hope.

As usual, he kept the radio tuned to KJR, the sport's channel, but he couldn't listen to another analysis of U-dub's upcoming football season. He switched the radio off.

Grayce thought he was still mad at her. He wasn't mad. He was afraid, afraid she'd never get past her fear of commitment. Still wounded by the loss of her sister, Grayce couldn't allow herself to trust the future. He felt that their love for each other should over-come the past. In Grayce's complicated mind, their love heightened the fear.

He didn't understand emotions like Grayce did, but what he did know was that he was afraid that she might never need him the way he needed her.

He had to make a stand. He couldn't allow her to wield so much power, but he worried that if he pushed her, she'd let him go... back to DC alone. So, he remained silent in a purgatory of his own making.

For three days, he had been unable to kiss her or even touch her. He was torturously aware of her every word, her every gesture, constantly hungering for every brief contact with her. It had gotten so bad that he watched her sleep. She didn't sleep well without him. She tossed and turned with a worried face. She was having night-mares, but she never admitted a word to him about her restless nights.

He tried hard to hide what she did to him in her little skimpy yoga clothes. He hadn't understood the power of obsession, had never felt its fierce pull until now. He couldn't reason himself out of this passion. He wasn't in purgatory. He was in hell.

CHAPTER THIRTY-THREE

Grayce sat in her usual chair, across from her mentor. The familiar fragrant scent of the Dragon Well green tea soothed her jangled nerves. There was comfort in routine. She smiled, then he smiled. Always the same, but never the same.

"How are you?" His fathomless eyes radiated love. She had come to be with him on the pretext of treatment for her concussion.

"I've a mild concussion from a car accident."

"Yes, I see the bruising."

"Someone had tampered with my brakes. My car went out of control, and I struck a tree. I was evaluated at Harborview. My CAT scan was negative. I've recovered. The men, possibly from Aunt Aideen's prediction, are still at large. Davis is trying to find a connection to why they want to harm me."

"Your mind is spinning, yes? Take a cleansing breath."

She took several deep breaths and tried to absorb Dr. Z's calm, but this time it wasn't working.

He smiled. "Still spinning. You remember the exercises we did when you first started your training?"

"That's the problem. My mind has taken hold of me, and I can't get out of its destructive grip."

"Your thoughts sound harsh. Lord Krishna reminds us in the *Bhagavad Gita* that gentleness of the mind must be practiced."

"Everything in my life is out of control, and I can't stop the whirling buzz."

"Yes, I can feel how disturbed your energy is. Tell me."

"I hurt Davis badly. And now we're distant. I don't know how to make it better between us."

"His fear over the accident, yes?"

"He's very upset that someone tried to hurt me. He's guarding me day and night."

Dr. Z never asked direct questions, but always waited for the truth to emerge.

"He's hurt because I didn't call him immediately after the accident. I didn't want him to worry. He was in DC on his new job, and I didn't want him to have to come home."

"You are used to taking care of others. Not easy for you to let someone else help you."

"He said I'm trying to push him away. But he doesn't understand that I wanted to spare him the pain."

"Your life journey has always been about preventing pain for others. There is more. I can feel it—a deeper fear than taking responsibility for others. What is it?"

She didn't want to admit her scary thoughts out loud, because uttering the words would make it real, never to be taken back.

Her mentor knew her mind so well, recognized her resistance. "Tell me about your dreams."

"Every night, it is the same dream or a slight variation. I dream I'm under water."

"Very auspicious. Water represents consciousness."

"But the dream isn't auspicious. I'm being suffocated by the water. And there is no one to help me."

His round eyes focused on her face. "Anything else?"

"I'm sinking into the emptiness alone. The anxiety is over-whelming."

"A very frightening dream. I can see why your energy is unbalanced. Deep fear of loneliness, yes?" His words always had the effect of softening the ache around her heart.

"Why do you think you're having this dream?"

There was never any hiding from her mentor. Dr. Z liked the analogy—delving deep into your soul is like peeling away one petal at a time from the lotus flower. He had never described the suffering involved in the process of peeling.

"Cassie's gone. She's left me. I used to feel her, dream of her, feel a connection. But when the men threatened me, I didn't feel her with me." Grayce couldn't hold back the anguish. Hot tears rolled down her face. Searing grief burned in her lungs. She gulped, trying to suppress the sobs.

Dr. Z leaned forward and patted her hand.

His touch steadied her. He never judged feelings. He allowed them to flow.

"Your sister didn't leave you." He put his hand on his chest. "Is she not here?"

Grayce shrugged her shoulders. "But if she is with me, why don't I feel her? Something has changed."

"I don't think she left you. I think you let Cassie go."

"That's not true!" She never totally lost control with Dr. Z, but today he was pushing her limits.

"You're letting go of very old fears in your dreams. And creating new dreams and hopes, yes?"

"I don't understand." Her voice was challenging, almost hostile.

"Cassie has always been a part of you. And she still will be. She is held deep in your heart. 'New beginnings are often disguised as painful endings.' My favorite poet Lao Tzu says it beautifully."

"By your reasoning, I should feel her presence more."

"We're back to the brain spinning. This isn't about reasoning. This is feeling."

Grayce felt the tightness in her chest and around her heart ease with acceptance.

"She will always remain a part of you, as will all the people you love. But you don't need her to be with you now to make you complete. Letting her go gives room in your heart for another who loves you and protects you."

Grayce stared at her mentor. "I'm not sure that I've room in my heart for both Cassie and Davis."

He shook his head. "Your brain is quite revved up today." Dr. Z's exuberant smile wreathed his face. "There is always room for love."

"But Cassie guided me. Helped me in my work."

"Your gifts of insight and intuition have always been yours and only yours. You're the gifted one. Cassie loved and protected you." He was always so patient, gently guiding her to painful truths.

"Am I substituting Davis for Cassie?"

He chuckled. "You need to stop your brain from talking. You can love Davis, because you have loved Cassie and let her go. The deepest love is always letting go."

He stood. "No more words. Come, I'll treat you now. Let me take care of you."

CHAPTER THIRTY-FOUR

D avis was slouched against the front of his parked car. Mitzi's head lay at his feet. The dog slept soundly, unfazed by her guard duty.

Grayce had been meeting with her mentor for over an hour.

Davis was restless. He had plans to talk with Gator's probation officer this afternoon. He was anxious to find the connection between the criminals and Grayce, and impatient to end the rift with Grayce.

When he heard the door open, he straightened and put his hand on the gun in his jacket pocket. He slowly turned in a circle. Mitzi continued to sleep unaware.

A little man in a brown robe, dressed like a monk, walked toward him. Grayce had never described her mentor as a monk. Davis was on shaky ground—he knew nothing about monks.

Davis was immediately struck by Dr. Z's resemblance to a shiny, brown nut with his bald head, brown eyes, and brown robe.

Mitzi jumped up and pranced toward the man as if she were greeting a familiar friend.

"Oh, Mitzi, very nice to meet you."

As with Grayce, Mitzi calmed promptly and assumed a position next to the monk as if she had been trained as his companion.

"And you must be Davis." Dr. Z's voice was soft but powerful.

Davis was used to men sizing each other up, establishing who was the biggest, fastest, and strongest. He was accustomed to being acknowledged as the alpha, the pack leader. This assessment was quite different. The man smiled with his whole face and looked deep into Davis' eyes, peering into his soul.

He suddenly felt very exposed. Did Dr. Z know about their fight? Had Grayce told Dr. Z about him going ballistic?

The man glowed as if the sunshine of the day came from within him. Davis found himself smiling back. The knot in his chest eased for the first time since Grayce's accident.

Mitzi sat at Dr. Z's feet. The monk rested his hand on Mitzi's head as if bestowing a benediction. "Mitzi is a very brave dog. Grayce has told me about her fierce devotion."

"Yes, Mitzi is very loyal to Grayce."

"I'm glad. Mitzi will help Grayce again."

Davis didn't like the sound of this. Too much like a prophecy. And though he didn't believe in that kind of stuff, it didn't mean he'd ignore it.

"But I don't want Grayce involved in dangerous cases."

Dr. Z nodded. "Yes, I understand your worry. Grayce has unusual gifts and must use them. A spirit like hers needs to be safe-guarded against the evils of the world. The universe has provided her with several stalwart protectors. I am reassured. You, Mitzi and your aunt will keep Grayce safe."

And with that, the little monk nodded, and walked back into his house. He turned and said over his shoulder as if an afterthought, "Grayce is sleeping. She is very tired from all the turmoil. You'll have to wait longer, Davis. Patience, Davis. Patience."

The little man had a twinkle in his eye. Davis knew that Dr. Z wasn't only talking about waiting for Grayce today.

But what did he mean by Aunt Aideen as Grayce's protector? Just like Grayce, her mentor spoke in riddles. Didn't anyone speak clearly and logically?

CHAPTER THIRTY-FIVE

Grayce left Mrs. Leary's house to retrieve Mitzi. The poodle had to remain in the car until Mrs. Leary gave permission to allow Mitzi to visit with Grendel, a sweet and silly Himalayan, Mrs. Leary's newest addition. Grayce was always fascinated by her client's choice of names. Mrs. Leary had taught English at UW and always chose her cats' names from the epic poem *Beowulf.*

Grayce was surprised that Mitzi had been so patient while Mrs. Leary had described her hospitalization in great detail.

Grayce had to do a lot of fast-talking to persuade Davis that this home visit was really essential, and she didn't need a bodyguard to visit an elderly woman. It helped that Davis had wanted to go down to the police station to look into Gator's criminal record.

Grayce wouldn't disappoint sweet Mrs. Leary. She wasn't about to cancel because Hunter Hines or Gator tried to intimidate her. Except for Aunt Aideen's prediction, she had no idea why either man wanted her dead.

She descended the steps from the sprawling house in the posh Laurelhurst neighborhood. A swift, vicious jolt of foreboding hit her right in the chest—the front door of her car was open and Mitzi was gone.

Trying to remain calm as her entire being was flooded with panic, Grayce scanned the spacious, manicured, English garden. She called and whistled for Mitzi. No response. Now, the metallic taste of fear was in her mouth. Her heart raced out of control. Grayce didn't want to alarm Mrs. Leary yet.

She ran down the winding driveway to the street. The house was hidden behind tall laurel hedges. When she came around the hedge to the street, a young, blond man with a polo shirt open at the neck was standing next to a black SUV with the passenger door open as if he was waiting for her.

"Get in." He spoke in an even, detached voice as if he were a pick-up car service.

Terror gushed from her pores. Desperate, she scanned the tree-lined street hoping to find help. Unfortunately, exclusive, orderly neighborhoods never have people wandering the streets.

"This is a mistake." It took a masterful effort to keep her voice calm, but her heart sped along like it would burst.

Although he had the expensive, casual look of Seattle's tennis club, he was dead serious. He grabbed her elbow. "No, you made the mistake when you started sticking your fucking nose into my business."

Grayce rolled to the balls of her feet, ready to chop her hand with a full force Tenkai move to dislodge his forearm.

His grip tightened. "Don't try anything or you won't see the poodle. And I won't say it again. Get in the car."

"Where's Mitzi?"

"Gator has the dog. And if you behave yourself, it will be safe."

She slid onto the passenger seat. She might have escaped by using her Aikido, but she couldn't let anything happen to Mitzi.

"What do you want from me?"

"Why have you been following me?"

"Following you? I don't even know who you are." She sounded desperate, almost hysterical.

"Listen, this day will get worse for you if you don't stop lying, bitch. Get me?"

"I'm not lying. I haven't been following you."

"Who was the solider with you in the *jungle?*"

"You were in the *jungle?*" The sensation of looking over the edge of a precipice hit her behind the neck and knees.

"All I have to do is call Gator, and he'll hurt the dog. So start again and tell me the truth this time."

"I want to see Mitzi before I tell you anything." Grayce noted that he drove over the Montlake Cut and merged onto i-5 south. She had left her phone in her purse with Mrs. Leary. She wondered how long it would take Mrs. Leary to call Hollie or the police.

"I'm not taking any chances with you fucking with my plans."

"How could I interfere with your plans? I don't know you or what you're doing."

She had been gripping the seat tightly, trying to master the primeval terror racing along her nerves.

He picked up one of her fingers and bent it backward slowly. Intense, agonizing pain shot through her hand. Her fingers were extremely sensitive.. It was as if this madman knew precisely how to hurt her.

"Cut the bullshit. I've had enough of your type of manipulative snooping for a lifetime. If you don't want the fucking poodle hurt, stop faking all the innocent crap."

"Let me see Mitzi."

"You want to see Mitzi?" He picked up his cell and showed her a picture of Mitzi—with a knife to her throat.

She felt nauseous. "How do I know that you haven't already hurt her?"

"You'll just have to trust me."

"Where are you taking me?"

"So many questions. You never stop, do you? I'm taking you for a little show. You're going to be impressed. Fireworks on Pier 69."

"To the waterfront?" There'd be hundreds of tourists at the waterfront. Escape should be easy, then she'd call Davis, but what would happen to Mitzi?

"I'm not taking you to the goddamn waterfront."

"Pier 69 is on the waterfront."

"Fuck, you are just like my meddling mother. Treating me as if I'm some dumb shit. I know the location of Pier 69."

She could feel his seething rage toward his mother, now directed toward her. And she was trapped in this car. Were they drug dealers? Grayce couldn't remember much of what Hollie had said about Gator except that he was brutal and despicable. She had been right. Gator was her pursuer and had tampered with her brakes.

"You work for Gator?"

"That's a joke. Gator works for me."

"I don't understand. I've only met Gator at Teen Feed when I was looking for a missing woman. What do you want with me?"

"Why was the solider with you in the *jungle?*"

Was it Angie that they wanted? Angie didn't have any memory of where and what she had done. Had she gotten involved in something criminal? Whatever Angie had gotten herself into, Grayce knew this guy was deadly.

"I was looking for a missing woman, but I'm not involved with law enforcement. I'm a veterinarian."

"I know who you are, Dr. Walters. The perfect Dr. Walters. " Again, the chilling sneer in his voice. "Graduated with honors from Cornell. Yes, I know all about you. And you just love meddling into other people's business." His perfect teeth, gleamed bright white, like out of a toothpaste commercial. "Now tell me who the solider was and why you were searching in *the jungle.*"

Their searching for Maddy had caused this disaster. They found only the map of Jack Block Park and kitty litter. Her heart thudded harshly against her chest with the dawning realization. This insane man was a terrorist and "fireworks" would be happening on Pier 69.

CHAPTER THIRTY-SIX

Davis kept watching the clock on the far wall. He was trapped in his second official Fusion Center meeting, which now was approaching three hours.

Grayce and Mitzi should be wrapping up their visit to Mrs. Leary. Since he'd discovered that Grayce's brakes had been sabotaged, he monitored every minute of her day.

She had promised to text him when she had arrived safely back at her office where Nick Welby and Talley stood guard. Of course, Davis knew Grayce's safety wasn't the only reason Nick stationed himself in the front office.

Grayce had refused to have the sergeant accompany her to her appointment. Grayce had put her foot down. There was only so much protection that she could tolerate.

His phone vibrated during the meeting, just loud enough for the presenter to hear. He turned toward Davis.

"Sorry for the interruption. I'm on-call for the department."

Grayce's office number appeared. Not sure why she was calling instead of texting. He'd be able to call in fifteen minutes, during the break.

Finally, after an overly detailed description of the statewide Integrated Intelligence System, Davis went into the corridor and called Grayce's cell. No answer. She was supposed to have her phone with her at all times. He dialed the office phone. Hollie didn't pick up.

There was a recorded message on the phone. Alarm shot through him. Where was everyone? He dialed Nick's cell.

The phone rang interminably. His heart hammered against his chest. The phone call from Grayce's office had been less than thirty minutes before. What had happened in the short time that no one answered? Sweat pooled on his back, on his hands and under his arms. He recognized the smell of fear. His imagination went wild. He had seen too much not to consider all sorts of deadly possibilities.

He called Grayce again as he sprinted to his car. He wondered if he should call the police. Grayce would be infuriated if she were seeing a patient and the police arrived.

Why wasn't Nick picking up his phone? What kind of bodyguard didn't respond?

He drove furiously toward Grayce's office, but he was twenty minutes away from Fremont.

He tried Nick's cell one last time before he'd call the police.

He could barely hear the phone ringing over the roaring pulse in his ears as he waited for Nick to answer. Panic was edging into his body. He kept trying to reassure himself that there must be a simple, plausible explanation. His experience as an investigator had taught him to trust his gut. Grayce was in trouble.

He picked up the phone to dial 911. The sound of his phone's ring startled him. It was Nick.

"Nick, what the fuck? Why haven't you answered?"

"We've got a situation, sir." Davis recognized the lethally calm voice that boded nothing good.

"What the hell does that mean?" He hated being talked to in that controlled manner.

"There is a bomb down on Pier 69, set to blow up the Port Commissioner's meeting."

"How the hell would you know that?" Davis' back went up—his mind was spinning—he needed to put his feet on the ground.

"Hollie and I discovered in the World of Warfare game that something big was going to happen so we came down here with Angie. Talley discovered the bomb."

"Where is Grayce?" Davis' voice got rougher as his lungs tightened in anxiety.

"We've been trying to call her at Mrs. Leary's to tell her about the meeting and that we were leaving the office. She hasn't picked up. Hollie said she's terrible about answering her phone. We've been calling her for the last hour. She should be finished with her visit by now. I then tried to call you, sir. And you didn't answer. And since we got down here, all hell has broken loose. The bomb squad is here, right now."

"Where is Grayce?"

"I don't know, sir. Hollie wants to speak with you."

"Davis." Hollie's voice was tremulous, the tough-ass street kid long gone. Davis was unnerved by the dramatic change. "We can't find Grayce. She isn't answering her phone."

Ugly, gross fear shook his body, as his adrenaline surged. "Give me Mrs. Leary's number."

"I don't have the number with me. I know we were supposed to guard Grayce, but I thought she was fine. I'm so afraid something happened to her."

"Calm down, Hollie."

"Wait, Davis."

Davis could hear Hollie speaking to another woman. He heard "Hunter Hines" and "military intelligence" and a shock quaked through him. He hadn't been able to find anything about Hunter Hines. Everyone in the digital age had a footprint unless they were a covert or a criminal.

"Davis, you still there? Maddy, Angie's friend, wants to talk with you. She has information. Here she is."

"Sir, I'll be brief. I've been working undercover with Hunter

Hines, tracking the leader of an ecoterrorist group. He's responsible for several bombing threats at military bases."

Davis' mind reeled with the implications of what Grayce had stumbled upon. "He planned the attack on Pier 69?"

"No, sir. It's a member of his group, a Brandon Billow, but we think that's an alias. He's been working with a guy named Gator."

"The guy who Grayce believed tampered with her brakes?"

"Yes, he is the same. I just notified Hunter of the bomb situation. He's been tracking Gator. And sir, Hunter witnessed Dr. Walters get into a car with someone he suspects might be one of Gator's associates. We don't have an ID on him yet."

"Why in the hell would Hunter allow Grayce to get into the car?" He knew the damn answer before he asked. If he were tracking a suspect, he'd want to glean as much information as he could before he called for backup.

"Sir, I know you're an investigator and have FBI clearance or I wouldn't be allowed to share this information. We're talking about a terrorist cell in Seattle. Hunter is following Dr. Walters and has put the FBI on high alert.

"Grayce is a hostage and all he's doing is following?" His anger spilled over, rushing into his entire being.

"We don't know if this man is connected to Brandon Billow or Gator."

"But you do know that Gator is connected to Brandon Billow who just tried to blow up Pier 69."

"Yes, sir."

"Give me Hunter's number. Which way were they headed? Do you have an ID on the car?"

"You'll have to ask Hunter about the car. I've been pretty busy here, sir."

"Where are they?"

"I-5 south. Sir, Hunter Hines will protect Dr. Walters at all cost."

Davis sped to the next exit to reverse his direction. He took the

45th street exit and raced down 1-5 south as he dialed Hunter Hines. The son of a bitch better pick up.

"Hunter Hines here."

"This is Ewan Davis. I just got off the phone with Maddy." Hell, he didn't even know the woman's last name. "You still have Grayce in your sight? I want backup called right now," he barked.

"The FBI has been alerted, but I don't want a major presence to alert the guy and spook him into rash behavior."

"Do you have eyes on Grayce?"

"Yes, she is in the front seat and appears unharmed. No force was used when she got into the car."

"What the hell?" Davis' mind raced. What could've made Grayce get into that car?

"When she freely got into the car, I first thought you'd hired private security. It was only by accident I saw her. I was following Gator, but lost him when he went down an alley."

"Where are you now?"

"I'm on 1-5 south by the 1-90 exchange. FBI is on stand-by waiting for the suspect's direction."

"I'm ten minutes behind you." Or less, if traffic didn't routinely back up in the downtown area. He drove eighty miles an hour, swerving around cars in every lane.

"Who is the guy who has Grayce?"

"I don't know, possibly Brandon Billow with an altered appearance. He doesn't match Maddy's description. This guy is clean-shaven, has a military look to him. What is his connection to Dr. Walters?"

"I wish I knew. It makes no sense. All I have is that Grayce was set up and you and Gator were following her before the accident."

"But why does this guy want Dr. Walters?"

"Hell, she was trying to help your mother. Everything else makes no sense. All I could find was that Gator was a lowlife thug, drugs, pimping, B and E. And, of course, your record has been swept clean."

"You're right about Gator. I have no idea how he's connected to ecoterrorists, but I have a feeling he's a gun for hire."

"Do you have an ID on the car?"

"A black Lexus SUV registered to a Meryl Billow on Mercer Island. Haven't been able to contact the owner, but I know that Brandon Billow is using his mother's car."

"Listen, he just exited to the West Seattle Bridge. I've got to call in the backup."

"I'm headed to the West Seattle Bridge, and I'll call you in less than five to find out where you're headed. And man, you answer the phone."

"Right."

CHAPTER THIRTY-SEVEN

Grayce kept her gaze on the road ahead, but out of the corner of her eye, she observed her captor. He looked like a regular guy, calm and in control, but she sensed his frenetic energy and how easily he could snap.

"I won't ask again. Now talk."

"I was searching for a missing woman on Beacon Hill."

"There's more to it." He leaned over to take her finger and waited.

Her entire body tightened in expectation of the approaching pain. "I was helping a client find her friend. That's all it was. Nothing else."

"Don't try to placate me." He dropped her hand. "You're just like her—always smoothing, always pretending."

At first, Grayce thought she could reason with him. Now, she realized he was both delusional and paranoid. "Are you talking about Maddy?"

"You can't stop, can you? Picking and prodding. Always trying to get everyone to do what you want. You're not going to manage me."

He gripped the steering wheel tightly. His dark eyes had a strange blaze, as if he was in his own world that was ready to explode.

"I'm sorry. I didn't mean to upset you." Her voice had become soft and soothing, the same voice she used when she was wary of an unpredictable animal.

"My God, you talk just like her. Looking down your nose on those of us who don't measure up to your superior standards. But today you're going to be looking from my perch."

Her heart struck sharp blows against her chest.

"You're gonna get to look down on the whole city from the park."

He needed Grayce to be part of playing out his fantasy. He wanted her to be impressed by his plan. In some weird, twisted way, he equated her with his mother.

"I'm not familiar with Jack Block Park, but I'm sure the views are spectacular." She had succeeded with an out-of-control, vicious Sun bear at the zoo. She could handle this obsessed, mentally ill man.

"How do you know where we're going?" His body stiffened, ready to strike.

She had made a huge mistake. Animals were much easier than people.

"Bitch, how do you know that we are going to Jack Block Park? Who else knows?" he exploded, his face red with rage, the veins bulged on his neck.

Grayce detected his musky smell, that of a cornered animal.

"When you turned off at Alki, I knew what park we were going to. There are no other parks at this exit."

He drove and turned in front of the large park sign partially obscured by trees and bushes. They crossed railroad tracks. He stopped the car part way down, hidden from the traffic, on the access road to the park.

"You just said you weren't familiar with Jack Block Park." His ominous calm was more frightening than his rage

"I've never been to the park, but I know of its existence. I grew up in Seattle."

"For lying to me, your stupid dog is going to pay."

He dialed Gator. "Put your phone on speaker. And kick the dog in the head. I want Dr. Walters to hear the poodle suffer."

"No, please. I'll tell you. Don't hurt Mitzi," she pleaded desperately. "I found a map of Jack Block Park in a sleeping bag."

His breathing deepened into aggressive surges. "You went through my sleeping bag?"

Never show your fear to a cornered animal. Fear breeds fear. "We didn't know it was yours, and we were hoping it belonged to Maddy."

"Gator, kick the dog."

Mitzi gave a keening cry that tore away all shreds of Grayce's composure.

"Brandon, do you want me to do it again?" Gator's humorous voice thundered in the car.

His name was Brandon. She searched her mind, but didn't remember meeting him.

"That's all for now." He turned toward Grayce. "Gator loves his job."

His smile was toothy and fiendish. She would have remembered someone so cruel. She had never met him. He never planned to release Mitzi. She had to escape. He had used the devoted poodle to trap Grayce in his sick game.

CHAPTER THIRTY-EIGHT

B randon drove a quarter mile on the access road in the isolated industrial area—an eerie landscape of Seattle's maritime past, too far from the main road for Grayce to break away. The wind blew off Elliot Bay, carrying dust from the dirt road across the windshield. Railcars covered with graffiti sat on the seldom-used track.

The shipping workers who moved the freight to trucks and trains had finished their work hours before. No one was around.

Railroad tracks protected by a ten-foot cyclone fence topped with barbed wire ran along one side of the access road. Puget Sound bordered the other. Over the high fence and over the tracks to Harbor Avenue was an unlikely escape route.

Brandon pulled into the parking spot in front of a welcome sign—Certified Wildlife Habitat. Two other cars sat in the far side of the visitors' parking lot—maybe she wasn't alone.

He turned off the ignition, then reached into the glove box, pulling out a large revolver.

Grayce backed against the seat, away from the shiny, lethal weapon.

"Afraid of guns?" His lip curled into a sneer. "I didn't think there was anything you'd be afraid of. Don't worry. I don't have plans to shoot you...yet." He laughed when she flinched. "My military school training comes in handy."

He tucked the gun into the back of his blue jeans, just like she had seen in the movies. "I learned a lot in military school, the same lessons I learned at home. Men use power to bend the weak to their will. And now the powerful men will bend to me." He checked his cell phone and his eyes gleamed with a cruel light. "Five minutes before show time."

He got out of the car and walked around to her door. She could kick him in the chest and make a run. But getting shot when trying to scale the ten-foot fence wasn't exactly a viable option. She was trapped for now.

He opened her door. "We're going to take a little walk up the hill for the view. You're going to witness how much I learned in my military school training. Impressive—what I've engineered."

Grayce scanned the area, searching for other routes of escape. The path was cut into a large hillside with dense trees on both sides and fences beyond to prevent access to the shipyard.

"Don't try anything funny. I won't hesitate to demonstrate my marksmanship. And I'd hate for you to miss the show."

Grayce shuddered. Icy fear ran down her spine rushing to her toes.

He gripped her elbow. "We have to hurry. Damn downtown traffic."

Brandon walked next to her, his gun tucked into his blue jeans. To hide his weapon, he wore a lightweight jacket embossed with a smiling penguin. They walked for at least a quarter of a mile. As they climbed, they caught views of the parking lots filled with trucks and boats on one side and views of the Sound on the other.

A teenage couple emerged, coming around the second curve on the path. They walked arm-in-arm, oblivious to everyone else.

Brandon bent toward Grayce and whispered in her ear as if they were also a couple. His hot breath on her skin sent chills of repulsion. "Don't think I won't hesitate to hurt anyone who tries to stop me and my plan."

Grayce stared at the couple. Little chance that they'd notice her dilated pupils, her swift breathing, or her sweaty palms.

Unaware of Grayce's distress, the couple disappeared around the next bend.

As Grayce and Brandon ascended higher, they had a panoramic view of Puget Sound. Jack Block Park was a peninsula that jutted into the Sound with a clear view of the Seattle skyline, the surrounding islands, Vigor Shipyards, and the container terminals.

"Do you see the seals?" He pointed among the barges.

Hordes of seals were lying next to and on top of each other on a floating buoy. More black heads bobbed in the water. Their high-pitched bark carried over the water.

"What do you think will happen to those seals with an oil spill?"

Grayce was horrified. An oil spill in Puget Sound? What was he planning?

"Do you think they care about the seals, the dolphins, all the marine life in Puget Sound? All they care about is the money."

How could she answer a deadly fantasy?

They kept climbing. Grayce was a bit short of breath from Brandon's rapid pace and the sharp incline. Brandon wasn't the least bit winded, which didn't bode well for any attempt to outrun him.

Brandon was in good shape, irrational, and armed. Her only chance against him was her Aikido. She had to wait for the perfect moment to use her less than hundred-pound weight against his two hundred pounds and his revolver.

Did Davis realize yet that she was missing? He had no leads to her disappearance, but she had total faith in his skills. It didn't look like he'd be in time for a rescue. She had to act soon.

Brandon pointed to an orange platform thirty feet off the ground eight hundred yards ahead. "Our viewing room." They began the walk up a winding path to the platform.

Brandon turned in a full circle when they arrived at the platform. "The view is perfect. I'd first thought I'd watch from a boat, but this angle is better. More dramatic with Mt. Baker as a backdrop." His body was coiled in expectation; his face twisted in excitement.

He had brought her here to witness a heinous atrocity. She still wasn't sure what the terrible deed might be.

Brandon checked his watch. "Three minutes. You're going to be mesmerized. I've seen videos of what the explosion will look like, but I keep visualizing it rather like a grand Hiroshima without the nuclear fallout."

"What do you hope to gain?"

"Exposing the authorities who've failed us. Do you know how many oil tankers and oil trains are coming into Seattle? Do you? Do you think the Port Commissioners care? They're in bed with the oil companies, stuffing their political campaigns with oil money."

"This is all about the oil tankers?"

"I'm sending a message to the men who treat people like they're nothing—not worth their time because they don't measure up."

"Why Pier 69?"

"Nothing gets past you—just like my mother. Very smart, Dr. Walters. Tonight is the Port Commissioners meeting."

"Why them? Why not target the oil companies?"

"They argue that they're bringing revenue into the city...they're bringing revenue into their pockets. And what's going to happen when Puget Sound is covered in an oil slick. Or one of those oil trains explodes near Golden Gardens? Will people care about the revenue?"

Her stomach twisted with his quixotic vision. Was he right?

"Look past the Ferris wheel. Those tourists are never going to forget their ride. It's going to be better than the Fourth of July over Elliott Bay. And like the celebration of our independence, this is another strike against the men who believe they can walk over the entire world. A few men controlling everyone's destiny. This will show them."

She shivered violently, abruptly cold with dread, nauseated from the inhumanity. How could she get away from his isolated spot and stop his malicious plan. "You're killing innocent people."

"It's the cost of doing business. See if the corporate devils like the *cost* when it involves them."

She kept hoping to wake up and be freed from this grisly nightmare.

"And we have front row seats."

"You'll never get away with it."

"My mother always had to point out the flaws in my thinking. Why my plans were *unrealistic*. Won't you both be surprised?"

He looked at his watch again. "One minute to D-day—been planning this for years."

Grayce was paralyzed. She couldn't jump off the thirty-foot platform. She couldn't disarm him unless he rushed her.

He walked her to the west side of the promenade. "Look down there. There's Gator and Mitzi waiting for us. I'll be taking a little boat trip—Vancouver Island, and then to Jakarta."

A large powerboat was moored at the dock below them. Mitzi was tied in the back seat.

He hadn't include Mitzi or her in his plans.

CHAPTER THIRTY-NINE

A fierce, battle-ready tension tightened every muscle in Davis' body. The rampaging need to harm the bastard thundered through him. He held the steering wheel in a sweaty, death-grip when the traffic slowed through the West Seattle Bridge interchange. The metallic taste of adrenaline saturated his taste buds. He'd give Hunter one more minute to call.

Finally, his phone rang.

Hunter spoke. "Davis, I've got you and FBI on speaker. The suspect exited Harbor Avenue. I continue to have eyes on Dr. Walters."

A stressed, controlled voice spoke. "This is Agent Andersen, FBI —Tactical Operations. Our hostage rescue team is fifteen to twenty minutes out. The Coast Guard is headed to Jack Block Park with an ETA of fifteen minutes. We've got to assume he's planning to escape by boat. There's a marina at Jack Block Park."

Davis knew nothing about the layout of Jack Block Park.

"Agents Hines and Davis. This is now an official FBI operation. You are to wait until our arrival. Do not proceed on your own. Do you copy that?"

"Yes, sir. Copy," Hines answered.

"This is a hostage situation with a possibly armed man. I don't want any dramatics. You are to await my orders," Andersen barked.

Davis' fear had been transformed into white-hot fury. "The hostage is my girlfriend. I'm not waiting around while that son of a bitch has her. Do you copy that?" His voice shook with rage. He slammed the phone down. He wasn't about to wait for the FBI, the Coast Guard, or any other bloody federal agencies.

He reached into the glove box and pulled out his service revolver. He wouldn't be hamstrung by bureaucracy.

His phone rang again. It was Hines.

"Davis, what the hell are you thinking? I need you to let me handle this. You're too emotional to function as my backup."

"I'm in total control. And I'm not waiting. This perp has a plan, and we need to intercept him before he gets Grayce on a boat.

"I agree. I'm in the parking lot. I've got eyes on the car, but no one is in it. I'm going to move toward the water and the dock where he'd have a boat secured. Are you armed?"

"Yes, Glock 30."

"By the map it's at least one quarter mile to the water, but no other escape routes."

"I'm turning into the park. Head to the water. I'm right behind you."

CHAPTER FORTY

"Ten, nine, eight..." Brandon held his cell phone to detonate the bomb, counting down the seconds remaining before Pier 69 would be blown to smithereens.

His deep voice boomed across the water. "...seven, six, five..." His glee in killing abraded her nerve endings, like nails clawing across a chalkboard.

Grayce's throat constricted. She struggled to breathe. She had a floating sensation, suspended as the world turned without her. She closed her eyes and prayed. Her helplessness was unbearable. With all her gifts and abilities, she hadn't been able to stop this horrific disaster.

"Three, two, one--bam!" His voice filled with exhilaration. His face beamed with excitement as he clicked the phone.

Grayce stared at Pier 69 waiting for the unthinkable. She ran her hands up and down her jeans, trying to bring herself into the present, contain herself from shattering.

Nothing.

The only sounds were the raucous seagulls overhead and seals on the buoy.

"What the fuck?" His face contorted into fury. His body coiled, ready to strike.

Grayce backed away. Like a baited, abused animal, he was ready to attack.

Her stomach rolled and dipped like the buoys below her.

He turned toward her. His hands gripped into white knuckled knots, his rage focused on her. "You did this."

"I did nothing. I would've if I had known, but I didn't know."

His eyes darted back and forth as he paced. "Bitch, tell me the truth or Gator will shoot the dog. Not enough to kill it—that would be too easy. But to make the poodle suffer as it bleeds out."

"Don't hurt Mitzi. All I ever did was try to find the missing women." She wasn't sure if it was the ferocity of her fear or the desperation in her voice that convinced him, but he backed away.

"I've got to get out of here. They'll start looking." He pulled his gun out of the back of his jeans. "Come on. And don't try anything. Remember, I've got nothing to lose."

The adrenaline pumped into her veins, driving her racing heart to a frenetic pace. She was edging toward full-blown panic. Instinct screamed to run. She tried to inhale, but her lungs were too tight to breath.

The cold nuzzle of the gun pressed through her t-shirt.

"Walk down the ramp."

Her mind raced for an escape. She could use the Tenkai movement to knock the gun out of his hand then run. He was wound up, frustrated and ready to react. He'd be able to outrun her and there was also Gator in the equation.

Her heart slammed against her chest and her mind was unfocused, like water rushing over a dam. She had to marshal her energy for the right moment—when he came at her. Aikido was using your opponent's energy against him. He was cornered and dangerous, and she needed to use his distraction. Mitzi would fight when Grayce moved into action.

He was inches away from her, with his gun prodding her back.

She could smell his desperation as the fear gushed out of his pores. She had to pull back and center her entire being for the coming confrontation.

"What are you planning to do with me and Mitzi?"

"I'm leaving you with Gator. I'm not a violent person." He pushed the gun against her back again when she slowed her walking. "But Gator's needs are a bit more exotic. You should have an interesting time with him. He wanted your assistant as part of the deal. I had to do some hard negotiating, but he finally agreed that your meddling might be interesting to overcome."

She was abruptly cold with dread, nauseated from it. Her concentration smashed.

"Keep moving." Brandon prodded her again with his gun.

It took all of Grayce's self-control not to turn and knock the gun out of his hand. Instead, she calmly walked onto the dock to the large twin inboard speed boat where Mitzi and Gator waited.

"Let me guess—your mother's?"

"She'll miss it more than she'll miss me, you bitch."

As soon as Mitzi spotted Grayce, she gave a whimpering cry. Gator, who sat behind the steering wheel, bellowed, "Shut up."

Revulsion shuddered through Grayce. Her entire body started to shake with the vicious violence she perceived in his face and eyes.

"The stupid-ass dog has been crying the entire fucking time." He turned and backhanded Mitzi. "Nothing shuts her up."

Mitzi, tied up on the back seat, growled at her tormentor.

Grayce's trembling intensified, driven by the need to retaliate. She couldn't allow impulsive reactions to rule. She needed to remain in control to escape.

Taking a shaky breath, she pulled her arms close to her side to stop the shivering and to assess her options. She eyed the angle in which she could lever her weight against Brandon to knock him into the water. Then she'd have enough time to run away before Gator could get out of the boat.

She could barely hear above the roaring beat in her ears as her heart sped recklessly.

"What the fuck is happening?" The fading sun reflected off the metal piercings imbedded in Gator's face. "Why didn't the bomb go off?"

"I've no idea. I've got to get out of the country. Every cop in the state will be looking for me once *Teresa* realizes that I put the bomb in her backpack. Sorry bitch thought she was carrying her camera."

"It should've blasted the entire city with the amount of RDX we used."

Grayce could feel the anxiety exuded from Brandon. Gator wasn't in the least upset by their failed plan and the jeopardy they were in if apprehended by the police. Grayce wondered if it was heroin or marijuana that kept him mellow. His drugged-out state was to her advantage.

Gator stood and climbed over the front seat. He threw a canvas bag on to the dock. "You got the car keys? I'm out of here."

Brandon kept the gun leveled at Grayce while he dug in his jean pockets to locate the keys.

Gator bent over Mitzi to untie her. Brandon, with gun in his hand, stepped with one foot on the boat to hand Gator the keys.

Immediately, Mitzi lunged at Gator's face. Her teeth were bared as she attacked. She knocked Gator backward against the back of the seat then jumped off the boat and ran to Grayce.

Crumpled on the floor. Gator screamed. "The fucking dog bit my face." He put his hand to his face to stop the bleeding. He stared down at his hand, covered in blood. "I'm going to kill that cocksucker." He struggled to stand.

Brandon's balance was precarious as the boat bobbed up and down. Brandon swayed between the dock and boat.

Grayce didn't have time for her careful Aikido plan—only time to react. She shoved Brandon as hard as she could from behind. The surprise and his precarious position sent him sailing face forward to the floor of the boat. His gun went off and hit Gator in the leg.

"You stupid fucker," Gator shouted. "You stupid fucker, you shot me."

Grayce sprinted with Mitzi following. She ran as fast as she could. She only had seconds before she knew Brandon would give chase. He wouldn't allow her to escape.

Grayce shot up the path. Her heart and legs pumped hard against the steep incline. All her senses were heightened. She noticed the sunlight flickering on the sidewalk, heard the seagulls overhead. Her over-wired nervous system waited for the gunshot.

Her heart pounded against her ribs. Her breath was short, but she pushed on. She cleared the open area and headed toward the protection of the greenbelt. She never looked back to see if Brandon followed. Mitzi ran ahead. There was no escape except the path to the parking lot.

The only sound was her hard spurts of breath. Mitzi bounced up the path as if on a morning jog. Grayce never slowed. The mix of fear and adrenaline kept her moving.

She panted through her mouth. She didn't waste any breath on reassuring Mitzi, who wasn't winded from her sprint or from the violent ordeal.

They came to the bend in the path where she had seen the young couple. Mitzi slowed and her ears went up. Grayce's heart slammed against her chest. She slowed her pace and listened. She heard footsteps ahead.

She jumped off the path into the wooded area. Mitzi turned and followed Grayce. They crouched behind a giant maple tree. She was panting and the rough sound echoed in the silence of the trees. Grayce had to swallow the sound of her wheezing. From their vantage point, Grayce could see the path.

She almost gasped out loud. She covered mouth with her hand, trying to suppress the fear that shot into her gut. Hunter Hines, with a gun in his hand, stealthily approached on the path. The sun glinted on the shiny metal of his revolver. Mitzi leaned against Grayce's leg.

She didn't know who to trust. She held her breath, afraid she might make noise if she breathed.

She waited behind the tree, listening for the shouts from Brandon or the fiendish Gator. There were no sounds and no signs of the men. She had to leave the hiding place, but she wanted to stay hidden, not risking exposure.

She listened and watched Mitzi's reaction to see if they were approaching. Nothing.

She slowly emerged from her hiding place then broke into a jog to the parking lot. She didn't have far to go. She'd wait in the trees before she ran down the totally exposed road to Harbor Avenue where people would be walking and riding their bikes, where there would be help.

CHAPTER FORTY-ONE

D avis sped down Jack Block's access road surrounded by abandoned rail cars and barbed wire fence. He was winded and sweating like a bloody race horse from his suppressed need for action. He methodically pulled air into his lungs and forced himself to focus on the mission. He couldn't allow himself to think about Grayce, kidnapped and brought to this desolate place by violent criminals.

He spotted the abductor's black SUV in the parking lot. Scanning the lot and his mirrors, he searched for any sign of the bastard. He rechecked his gun before he jumped out of his car and ran to the trailhead.

A surprised shout made his back muscles flex involuntarily. "Davis, what are you doing down here?"

Wound tight, Davis reeled around with his gun leveled.

"What the...?" Roger Burdrick backed away.

Davis recognized two men walking toward him, wearing SFD issue sweats: Roger and Scott, fire fighters from the West Seattle station. Davis signaled them to be quiet with a cutting motion across his neck.

Both men nodded, approaching in silence.

"What the hell are you two doing here?" Davis whispered.

"We're finishing our check of the commissary." Roger pointed to Harbor Avenue where the fire department maintained a storage area of surplus equipment. "Then we use the hill to do part of our workout, but not today with the bomb threat. We're waiting on orders." He pointed to the winding path leading up the hill. "Are you following a lead on today's threat?"

"Yes, the bomber is armed and holding my girlfriend hostage. We think he's going to make a getaway by boat and take her with him. A federal agent is ahead of me. I need you to cover my back," Davis said.

Trained for every kind of emergency, the firefighters gave the thumbs-up, battle ready.

"Davis, I can go with you. Roger can stay here," Scott said.

Davis, already heading up the path, turned briefly. "You're unarmed. Stay here. Make sure no one leaves the area. FBI is five to ten minutes out. Be careful—this guy is dangerous."

From the hill above, Davis heard a distinctive yelp. "Mitzi?" He called out in a hushed tone as he sprinted toward the sound.

He kept his gun level.

"Davis. Oh, my God. Is it really you?"

He heard Grayce's voice coming from a stand of trees.

Suddenly, he saw Grayce emerging from the woods with Mitzi by her side—both safe and unharmed. Overcome with relief, he felt shaky, like trekking on K2 at twenty-four thousand feet without an oxygen tank.

"We've been hiding in those trees since we heard men's voices coming from the parking lot." Grayce's hair was disheveled, her blue jeans and blouse smeared with dirt. He saw no evidence of assault. Mitzi seemed her usual energetic self, prancing next to him.

With one arm, he lifted Grayce against his chest and pressed her tightly. "Thank God. Are you all right?" He looked down at her smudged face. Dreading the question that had his gut twisted into knots, he asked. "Did he hurt you?"

"No, I'm fine, but it was awful." Her usual bright eyes were flat, her plucky voice unnatural.

He lowered her to the ground. "Where is the bastard?"

Grayce spoke in a low undertone. "They're at the water on a boat. We've got to get away."

"They?"

"Gator and a guy named Brandon. And Hunter Hines went toward the water with a gun in his hand. He's not one of them, is he?"

"Hunter Hines is a Fed."

Grayce shook her head. "We've got to get away. They'll be coming after me."

Davis had one arm around Grayce's shoulder, holding her next to him as they descended down the path. Mitzi walked next to them. He still had his gun in his other hand, not taking any chances. "There's no time to explain. I need you to wait in my car until the FBI gets here. There are two fire fighters in the parking lot to protect you."

"But who's going to protect you?" She kept her arm wrapped around his waist. If he weren't wound so tight, he might have laughed.

Gunshots erupted behind them. He grabbed Grayce's arm and dragged her behind a tree. Mitzi leapt next to Grayce and positioned herself between Grayce and the path. "Get down and stay down," he commanded in a hushed voice. "Mitzi, stay."

With his Glock drawn and ready, Davis peered around the tree to see a blond man, holding a gun, running toward them. The man leapt off the path and crouched behind a tree. Davis lost sight of the man.

Hunter Hines, in a bulletproof vest, suddenly came around the corner from the path above.

Davis shouted, "Look out, Hines."

A shot rang out.

Hines dropped to the ground and rolled toward the trees.

Davis sprinted toward the shooter, but couldn't get a clear shot as the attacker ran full speed back up the slope in the woods.

An uninjured Hines quickly jumped to his feet and ran toward Davis. He was out of breath, disheveled, but maintained formidable control.

"I followed the bastard as he ran down the path. Did Dr. Walters get away? Where is she?"

"She's right here."

Grayce and Mitzi came from behind the tree.

"Thank God, Dr. Walters, that you're safe. Was that the man who abducted you?" Hunter asked.

"Yes. His name is Brandon."

"Brandon Billows," Hunter said.

Hunter turned toward Davis. "Get her and the dog away from here. I'll follow the perp. He's going to try to get back to the boat."

Grayce placed her hand on Hunter Hines' arm. "You can't go alone. Brandon has a very violent accomplice. Gator is wounded and in the boat."

Davis couldn't listen to Grayce's distress. Rage surged through his body, the overwhelming need for revenge pulsed in every cell. He struggled to keep his head clear.

"Thank you for the warning. I'll track him, but I won't do anything until help arrives. Now that you're safe, I'll let the FBI and Coast Guard catch him. I was desperate when I thought he had you," Hunter said.

Grayce said in a quiet voice, "Thank you."

Davis wrapped his arm around Grayce, "I'm right behind you, once I get Grayce into a safe place."

After the hell they'd both been through, Davis didn't want to leave her, but he had to make sure that bastard was put away or put down.

Davis, Grayce, and Mitzi hurried down the last incline and around the bend to the parking lot where Scott and Roger had positioned themselves at opposite ends.

The fire fighters came running. "We weren't sure what to do when we heard the gunshots. We stayed in position to make sure the bastard didn't get away," Scott said.

"You did the right thing," Davis said.

Roger stared at Grayce in disbelief. "How did you save her so fast?"

"I didn't." Davis pushed her hair away from her eyes. "She and Mitzi saved themselves."

Davis clamped his hands on her shoulders, hesitant to let go. "I need you to wait here until the FBI arrives. Roger and Scott will watch out for you."

He tucked his gun into his jacket, dug out his car keys, and handed them to Roger. "There are blankets in my trunk. She's had a shock."

Davis ran his hands up and down Grayce's arms. "Honey, get in the car with Mitzi. Wrap up in the blankets and rest."

"How am I supposed to rest while you're chasing those men?"

"Grayce, you'll be safe in the car with Roger, Scott, and Mitzi on guard."

Davis pressed a hard kiss against her lips. "I'll be back soon."

She touched his face reverently. "Davis, be careful."

He started to close the car door, then, hearing squealing tires, turned to look. "Thank God. The cavalry has arrived."

Four black SUV's came racing down the access road, then swerved and surrounded his car.

Davis had took out his wallet, which contained his ID, and lifted it and his free hand into the air. He glanced at Scott and Roger, who looked at him with moon eyes. "Hands up lads," he cautioned. Roger and Scott obeyed, looking like boys who had gotten caught cutting class by their sadistic vice principal.

The leader, heavy-set, with a square jaw, barked, "Step away from the car. Show me your hands."

Davis shook the wallet in his hand to draw attention to it. "I'm Captain Davis, Seattle Fire Department. Are you Agent Andersen?"

The agent stepped around Davis and spoke to Grayce. His gun was now pointed at Grayce. "Ma'am, are you Dr. Walters?"

"I am. Please tell your men to stop pointing their guns at us. Captain Davis is here to help."

Davis had taken out his wallet and provided the necessary ID.

Andersen leaned forward to talk to Grayce. "Are you injured, Dr. Walters? Do you need medical attention?"

"I'm fine, thank you. The man who abducted me is on his way to the dock on the other side of the hill. He's about to escape by boat. Hunter Hines is up there alone."

Andersen gestured to four of the men to start up the hill. "How did you rescue her, captain?"

"She escaped on her own, but I don't know the details. We need to help Hines who is on his own with the two armed guys."

Andersen pointed to the north end of the parking lot. "Close off the perimeter, Buckley. And close down the road. Block off all access in and out of the park."

He pointed to another agent. "Get the civilians out of here. Take them to the end of the road."

Davis started to follow Andersen. "Davis, you're finished here. You wait with Dr. Walters for questioning. This is an FBI operation."

Davis sat in the FBI's SUV with Grayce nestled in his arms. His heart hammered against his chest; he consciously tried to slow his speeding heart. It took all of his self-control to sit and wait. He'd been left behind while the FBI agents and Hunter Hines got to take down the bastards. He wanted to be the one to capture the scum. What he really wanted to do was kick the shit out of them for terrifying Grayce.

Wrapped in a blanket, Grayce had become very quiet. She hadn't spoken since they had entered the car. Mitzi slept on Grayce's feet, trying to warm her.

Color was coming back into Grayce's face. He didn't probe about her abduction since he knew she still faced grueling questioning by the FBI.

He did the only thing he could do. He held her and tried to soothe their jagged emotions. He ran his hand along her back, kissing the soft whisper of hair surrounding her face. She hadn't stirred for ten minutes, and he wondered if she was asleep.

Finally, Agent Andersen and Hunter, strutting like roosters, came down the hill, both grim but pleased. Brandon and Gator were both handcuffed. Gator had a shirt tied around his leg, but walked unassisted. Agents escorted the bastards, one on each side.

Grayce's entire body tightened when the pair walked past.

"Don't look at them, honey. I'm sorry I didn't protect you."

Grayce shook her head. "It wasn't your fault. You didn't want me to go to Mrs. Leary's alone. I underestimated how evil they are. They're just kids really. Like Hollie and Angie."

He didn't know how he would do it, but he was determined never to let anyone harm this compassionate woman. His job was to be the guardian of her special light.

"I'm glad that you were spared confronting Brandon and Gator," Grayce said.

Davis suppressed a grimace. She still didn't understand him, nor the male need to decimate the enemy.

She looked up into his eyes. Her eyes were wide and fathomless." I know you wanted to chase them, but I'm glad you didn't. Being exposed to the violence takes a toll on your soul."

Or maybe she did understand.

CHAPTER FORTY-TWO

D avis pulled up in front of Grayce's house. Several cars were parked in the driveway. All the lights in the house were on. Davis saw James' red Beamer and a green Ferrari which looked quite a bit like his aunt's. It couldn't be his aunt's car. Aunt Aideen wouldn't have known about Grayce's ordeal, and she didn't know where Grayce lived.

Grayce was tucked under his arm, sleeping soundly. He drove with one hand steadying Grayce so she wouldn't be disturbed. Mitzi was fast asleep in the back seat.

The questioning by Agent Andersen had been grueling for both of them. Grayce had to recount repeatedly all the details while he had to listen to the grisly nightmare. A nightmare that he was unable to prevent or stop. It made a man humble and raging at the same time.

He didn't want to wake Grayce. He was selfish. He didn't want to share her with her friends and family. He wanted her all to himself, to hold, and wipe away every one of her tears.

He kissed Grayce on the soft, tender spot in front of her ear and whispered. "We're home, sleepy head."

Grayce murmured something under her breath but didn't stir.

"Honey, you want me to carry you into the house?" That always got a reaction.

Grayce sat up and opened her eyes. "I can walk. I'm fine."

Grayce didn't like his tendency to bundle and cart her around. She had refused his offer to carry her to the car after the FBI interrogation. She had no desire to be treated as if she were a damsel in distress. She didn't understand that he needed to hold her. He needed the comfort. It wasn't every day that a man felt totally helpless.

"I think you've got company."

The front door opened and a crowd streamed out onto to the front porch. Davis saw James and Hollie and, damn it, Aunt Aideen. Who had told her? Two women stood next to his aunt that he didn't recognize. He assumed that the women were Angie and Maddy, the two missing Marines. Hunter Hines stood behind the women.

Nick, and Talley stood with Hollie. And obviously the other couple were Grayce's parents, with Grayce's mom an almost identical match to Grayce.

Grayce and Mitzi both bounded out of the car. The group cheered as Grayce rushed into her mother's arms. Grayce's dad encircled both women in a warm embrace. Mitzi sat next to the reunited family. Tears poured down Grayce's mother's cheeks. Her dad furtively wiped away a tear. Everyone grew silent with the family's touching reunion. James was wiping tears from his eyes with a polka-dot handkerchief.

James turned to the group, "Let's break into the champagne I brought. It's time to celebrate."

The group followed James into the house.

Davis hung back from the family, uncertain what his part should be. Finally, Grace turned and beckoned him over.

"Mom and dad, this isn't the way I hoped for you to meet Davis." Her voice choked up.

Davis stepped onto the porch.

Grayce's mom had clear hazel eyes, not as green as Grayce's. She wore high heels which didn't make up for her size—as tiny as Grayce.

"Davis, I'm so pleased to finally meet you. I'm sorry that my work prevented Tom and I from having you over for dinner. I promised Grayce that once I got the grant finished, I'd have you over. Grayce explained the deadline, didn't she?"

Grayce's teeth bit into her lower lip.

Mrs. Walters had her arm still around Grayce's shoulders. She squeezed a bit harder. "Grayce Ann Walters, you didn't explain about my deadline? The poor man probably thinks that we never wanted to meet him."

"Mom, I'm sorry. Your schedule never came up."

"No harm done, Christine. We're meeting him now." Mr. Walters turned toward Davis. His face was warm with a broad smile. He extended his hand.

"Davis, my mother has been out of the country writing a grant with other researchers and has been unable to have you for dinner."

"Very funny, miss smarty pants," Grayce's mother chided.

Grayce looked at Davis. Her lips were parted, and her eyes glinted with a mischievous glow.

"It's a pleasure to meet you, Davis." Mr. Walters gave a firm handshake and looked directly into Davis' eyes. This moment was as intimidating as meeting Dr. Z—the other important man in Grayce's life. "You look like the kind of fellow that might be able to handle Grayce's interesting talents and her wild adventures."

Davis wanted to tell Grayce's father that this last adventure had aged him, but he didn't wish to subject Grayce's parents to the violent craziness that their daughter had experienced.

James came out on the porch with two glasses of champagne. James passed the full coupes to Grayce and to her mother. "I think you need this, before Grayce tells of her latest misadventures."

"There really isn't that much to tell, James." Grayce was giving James a disapproving look which he predictably ignored.

"Nice try, Grayce." James moved next to Mr. Walters. "Tom, I brought a bottle of Scotch since I know you're a Scotch drinker. I wish I could report that Grayce has a full bar, but your choice is Champagne or Scotch."

"Scotch it is."

"Come into the house, and I'll pour you 'a wee-dram." James did his best imitation of Aunt Aideen's sham Scottish brogue. "Davis' aunt is making headways into the Scotch." James put his arm around Christine's shoulder. "Your shoes are divine. Are they Louboutin?"

"No they're Sophia Webster. She's a British Designer. Do you think they're too young for me?"

"Never, Christine. The shoes are ageless, like you."

Christine tittered, and Tom shrugged his shoulders at James' exaggerated gallantry.

After everyone had moved inside, Davis stepped closer to Grayce, wanting to pull her into his arms. He restrained himself. He was feeling very shaky about all he had experienced in the last seventy-two hours. He didn't know if he could live through another day like today.

Grayce took a sip from the glass. "James has the best taste in everything. Fabulous French champagne." Her lips were moist, and all he could think about was licking the essence off her plump lips.

"Did you see my parent's eyes? Pure relief. I feel badly that I've put them through another stress."

"Honey." He no longer cared about the guests. He wrapped his arms around Grayce, inhaling her sweet scent. "All I saw was two parents who love their daughter."

He kissed the fine little hairs around her forehead. "They're your parents. They don't want you to protect them."

"But when Cassie died, I felt like I was required to make them happy."

"Your parents are happy. They're grateful to have a daughter to love after losing one."

Grayce leaned against him. She wrapped her arms around his waist and snuggled close to his chest.

James opened the screen door. "Grayce, everyone is waiting for the guest of honor and for a recounting of today's adventure."

Davis bent down and whispered. "We'll talk later, honey. We'll straighten all this out. I love you, Grayce."

"Ditto, Davis." Grayce giggled. "I like the sound of 'Ditto, Davis'." She tittered. "I don't think I should be drinking champagne when I'm so tired."

"If you don't behave, I'm going to have to carry you."

"You're such a brute." She melded her body against his and pressed her wet lips against his. "My brute."

Grayce was ebullient. She was grateful to be surrounded by the people and animals she loved. She resolved on the spot that she'd be better about including them in her life.

Hollie rushed up before Grayce could get through the doorway. "Boss, it's my fault. Nick and I should've stayed at the office."

Nick walked over and put his arm around Hollie. He looked down at her with a sweet look of caring. Hollie was captured in his stare. Clearly, Grayce wasn't the only one who had an interesting day.

"I'm sorry Dr. Walters, but I don't think it would've made a difference if we had stayed at the office. Brandon Billow followed you to Mrs. Leary's. When Hollie and I found the chat about the group meeting at Pier 69, we had to act."

"You three stopped a bomb from exploding. The FBI agent told me how Talley uncovered the bomb that was in one of the protestor's backpacks. Obviously, our heroine is tired from her adventures."

Talley and Mitzi were sleeping side-by-side in the center of the room.

The champagne and exhaustion began to catch up with Grayce, who was already feeling giddy. Her hand wobbled when she raised her glass. "I want to make a toast to our heroes and heroines. Everybody raise your glass to thank them for preventing a disaster today."

Nick's cheeks colored a bright red. Hollie beamed up at him. Angie and Maddy raised their glasses to Grayce. Hunter Hines gave a slight nod.

Talley continued to soundly sleep, as did Mitzi. Perhaps dogs had better sense than the rest of us—p sleeping when exhausted and foregoing the champagne and parties.

Davis was talking to his aunt. He wasn't pleased by whatever she had said. She probably was telling him about the prediction.

James raised his glass. "And to the person who started the whole adventure. Without her, Angie wouldn't have been found, the plot to bomb the waterfront wouldn't have been foiled, and Grayce wouldn't have been abducted. Let's raise our glasses to our dear friend... Emily Chow."

Everyone said in unison. "JAAAAAMES."

And then everyone started to laugh.

Grace looked around at the full circle of family and friends. It was right to share this moment with them.

"You're up, Grayce." James waggled his eyebrows. "We've heard about the bomb on Pier 69, but we don't know the details of your day."

Grayce took a gulp of champagne. Sharing her experience with the people she loved would be a challenge.

"You have to understand..." She looked at her parents and Davis. "All I ever wanted to do was help Mrs. Hines. Then events got tangled and convoluted. I don't expect that I'll understand the whole chain of events for quite a while. I thought Hunter was behind the plot." Hunter Hines smiled at Grayce. The first time she had seen him smile. Everyone chuckled as if it were a joke, then waited expectantly for her to continue.

"It was all a fluke that Brandon Billow observed me at the house on 65th and then again on Beacon Hill. He was part of the ecoterrorist group and planned the real bomb. Although he planned to kill the

Port Commissioners, he never planned to hurt me. What Agent Andersen explained to me in my debriefing was that Brandon became obsessed with me. I somehow represented his mother, and he wanted me to witness his crowning achievement. He apparently wanted to impress me and never had plans to harm me. I was never in any real danger."

James rolled his eyes, knowing exactly how she was avoiding stressing her parents. Davis' warm eyes and crooked smile showed his support. He understood and accepted her need to protect the people she loved.

Aunt Aideen stepped forward, a glass of Scotch in her hand. "Grayce, you didn't start the story at the beginning. The adventure all began with a prediction."

All eyes turned toward Aunt Aideen. Grayce began to worry, uncertain what Aunt Aideen would share.

"I read Grayce's tarot cards and predicted she would go on a dangerous adventure, and, in the end, she and Davis would protect each other, and strengthen their relationship. The cards never lie. Am I not right?" She looked directly at Grayce.

Grayce shared a moment of harmony with Aunt Aideen. She and Davis had come through danger and hurt and were stronger by the journey.

"I'd like to make another prediction," Aunt Aideen said.

Davis and Grayce shouted simultaneously. "NO!"

The large woman gave a belly laugh. She raised her glass of Scotch. "All I was going to say is 'A h-uile là sona dhuibh's gun là idir dona dhuib which means 'long life will come to all in the room'."

CHAPTER FORTY-THREE

Davis was agitated, impatient. The party dragged on, taking way too long to break up. The obvious attraction between Hollie and Nick made him envious. He wanted to be alone with Grayce. It was time for the guests to take the hint and leave.

James acted as host. Somehow, he had organized amazing food and drinks for the party with essentially no notice. He even had party napkins that said, "People say 'High Maintenance' like it's a bad thing."

Didn't anyone else notice that Grayce was exhausted? Her color was wan, and she had dark circles under her eyes.

Grayce was running on fumes, but she took time to connect with each person. Everyone had to retell his part in the dangerous adventure. Although James didn't play an active role in the rescue, he didn't shy away from center stage in his dramatic description of casing the condemned house on 65th and doing reconnaissance with Angie on Beacon Hill, discovering two vital clues—the map of Jack Block Park and the kitty litter.

His aunt and Grayce sat huddled together on the couch, talking in whispers. Aunt Aideen held Grayce's hand and patted it lovingly. He couldn't hear what they were saying, but it was emotional for both of them.

After an excruciating two hours, everyone finally left. Grayce stood on the porch waving to her parents. Davis wasn't sure if they grasped the danger their daughter had endured, but they seemed to understand that Grayce needed their reassurance.

Davis came from behind and pulled Grayce securely against him. "Honey, let me run a hot bath for you." Her soft curves pressed against him, sending a wave of heat through his body.

He'd need all of his self-control to act like a gentleman toward Grayce tonight. She needed gentle, nurturing care after the shock she'd sustained; he needed to take them both on a wild, rough ride. He held himself in check, but his need to express his feelings in the most primitive, male way was intensifying.

She turned in his arms and looked up at him. "You and James were right. I need to let people take care of me, too."

She sighed and ran her hand along his jaw. "You need a shave, but I love your scruffy look."

"Because I remind you of your canine patients." Her touch and scent were doing crazy things to his heart rate. His breathing deepened to violent rushes.

"I'm impressed with your restraint tonight."

"My restraint?" Did she already know that he was seconds away from ripping her clothes off?

"You're dying to read me the riot act."

"Kind of..."

He never wanted to feel as helpless as he did today. Never wanted her to be in danger's way.

She laughed. The joy in her laughter went down his spine into his bones. Her lightness made the darkness of the day disappear.

"It can wait." He wasn't going to talk about the dangers tonight. With the memory fresh in his mind that Brandon had planned to give

Grayce to Gator, his fear was building to white fury. "You need a hot bath...and a Diet Coke."

"I do want a hot bath. And a Diet Coke would hit the spot. But after tonight's harrowing experience, I have only one need." She kissed the pounding pulse in his neck, driving sharp blows inside his chest.

"You do?" He was breathless, as if he had just climbed Mt. Rainier. He was waging an internal battle with his self-discipline.

"Grayce, you don't understand. You deserve a considerate lover tonight. You were in shock. And I'm not sure I have the restraint."

She had been rubbing herself against him as her hands made circles on his back. The exquisite sensation was driving him mad. Suddenly she stopped.

"I wasn't in shock."

"You wouldn't know if you were in shock. You were shivering and you couldn't speak."

"I was shivering from the overload on my nervous system. And I consciously chose to become still, trying to release the violent energy from my body."

"I'm sorry you had to be exposed to those bastards."

"I confront evil in my work all the time." Her fingers played with the buttons on his shirt.

"Your work is healing animals."

"I deal with cruelty way too often. I've taken care of many abused animals. They're innocent victims of rage. I have to release the negative energy or I can't heal."

He wasn't sure he was following the conversation. He didn't totally buy the stuff about absorbing energy. He knew how he dealt with dirt bags like Brandon and Gator, but Grayce wouldn't want to hear his aggressive tactic.

Grayce melted against him. "I realized when we sat in the car together that we make the perfect couple." She put her hands under his shirt, circling her fingers on his chest over his nipples.

"What?" He could barely get the words out.

"Sitting next to you in the FBI car, I realized that your presence acted like a shield to protect me."

"I will protect you forever."

"I know, Davis. And you know what else I know."

He could hardly focus since Grayce's fingers spread heat and fire as they wandered to his back and further down his lower spine.

"I need to be your shield, too. Protect and take care of your needs. And you have an incredible need."

Somehow Grayce hands were on the front of him. There was only so much a man could take.

"Didn't you hear anything I was saying?" His voice was gruff. "I can't be gentle tonight."

"I don't need gentle. I need you. I need the touch of a good man."

He held her face between his hands. Trembling with passion, he kissed her slowly and deeply. He wanted to take care of her, make her delirious with the same pressing need. He kissed her voraciously. She tasted of goodness and woman.

Breathless, she responded enthusiastically. Her hands moved up to the back of his neck, spreading her fingers into his hair. She pulled him closer and plunged her tongue into his mouth.

His heart pounded a demanding beat through his body.

Lifting her into his arms, he carried her into the bedroom. He put her down beside the bed. He began to undress her, but she kept kissing him as she struggled to get out of her blouse and bra. He helped her unzip her blue jeans.

When he saw the little wisp of lace above her blond tight curls, his control vanished. His hands and body started to shake in need. He squeezed her nipples, tightening them into hard buds as he kissed the soft hollow of her stomach. His tongue made a path to her curls. He needed to taste her. He pulled her jeans down.

"Grayce, lie back on the bed."

Her eyes were filled with desire. Her lips swollen and her breath coming in short bursts.

Tremors of need careened through his body.

A dazed Grayce lay back on the bed. He positioned her the way he wanted her—open. "I want you open for me. I'm ravenous for the taste of you."

He knelt before her. He slowly pulled her lacy panties down. The sweet scent of his woman made his erection throb. He wanted to make it good for Grayce, but he could barely hold onto to his control.

He trailed kisses down each thigh, her earthy scent beckoning to him. He rubbed his unshaven chin along her thighs. She responded to the abrasive sensation. Each time he rubbed her thigh she made a deep mewing sound, an overwhelming seductive sound that demanded him to thrust into her.

He teased her. He traced the outer sides of her labia with his tongue, but not touching her swollen, erect nub. She tasted of salt and mystery.

"Davis," Grayce pleaded in a soft whisper.

He ran his tongue along her heat, pulling softly, circling with his tongue.

"Now." Grayce grabbed Davis' head and pulled him closer.

"Is this what you want?" He swirled his tongue and then began to lick, thrusting his tongue into her.

He felt her tighten and spasm around him. He kept his tongue on her clitoris, feeling the pulsation.

"Davis, I need you now." A demanding Grayce made him very happy.

Desperate to be deep inside her, he pulled his shirt over his head and tugged his pants off in record time.

He covered her with his body, nudging her legs further apart. He settled himself between her thighs and pressed slowly into her. Burying his face into the side of her neck, he groaned in sheer bliss. "You feel so good. So tight."

He was trying to control his need, but he couldn't wait. He slipped his hands under her hips, lifting her to him, thrusting into her. He plunged a little deeper, edging to ecstasy.

He stroked the need in her until she was writhing beneath him and pleading for more. Her moans urged him on. She dragged her nails along his back. All restraint was gone. He was more forceful penetrating deeper, quickening the pace of his thrusts.

She cried out as her orgasm consumed her. "I love you, Davis."

He lunged again and again, groaning his love for her as his seed spilled inside her, shuddering uncontrollably with the force of his release.

Davis collapsed onto her, unable to move or speak. He pushed the hair away from her face. He wanted to see her eyes. She had said she loved him. He wanted to hear the words again.

Grayce was sound asleep.

"I love you, Grayce Walters, and I'm never letting you go." He kissed the tiny wisps of blond hair along the side of her face. He rolled off of her and pulled her into his arms.

She snuggled closer in her sleep and murmured, "We're perfect."

EPILOGUE

Davis and Grayce approached the backstage door at The Kennedy Center in Washington DC. Grayce's fingers were linked with Davis. After the kidnapping, Grayce and Davis both were taking time to savor their love.

"I can't believe we're getting a backstage tour. Wasn't it sweet of James to arrange?" Grayce asked.

"I'm convinced that James was more traumatized by your experience than you were," Davis said.

"He does have an amazing imagination, and I suspect he's filled in the less dramatic moments with terrifying details."

"He took me aside and instructed me to forbid you from investigating missing persons, terrorist plots, and the Russian mob. He had quite a list."

"And what did you say?"

"I told him that I continue to have nightmares, and that I'm thinking of joining the FBI to be able to protect you better." Davis's voice had adopted a no-nonsense tone, but his bright eyes glinted with mischief.

"Very funny. What did you really say?"

"I told him that we had come to a mutually satisfying arrangement about each other's work and interests." He looked down at her, his eyes brimming with smoldering hunger. "Of course, I didn't tell James how satisfying our agreement is. But as you said, James does have a great imagination."

The knowledge of their lustful intimacy reflected in his eyes, caused heat to curl in her stomach and then move into her chest and face.

"I'm not up for James' wisecracks right now."

"Honey, I love the way you blush. Makes me want to skip the ballet and take you home."

"Oh, no. I'm not missing a performance of the American Ballet Theater. They're my favorite ballet company, after Seattle's company, of course. This would be like skipping out in the third inning when Felix Hernandez's pitching."

"Whatever you want, I'm just happy to have you to myself for an entire week. I did speak with Hunter Hines earlier today. Do you want to hear his update, or would you rather not think about it tonight?"

"I want to hear," Grayce said.

"Brandon Billow's lawyer is pleading insanity. Like being bad and disappointing your rich parents is mental illness. Brandon knew full well that he was doing something criminal, an "insanity defense" isn't going to fly—but Hunter thought he might cut a deal with a prosecutor."

"He's not going to prison?"

"Oh, he's going to prison, but for how long is the question. Gator —well he's on his own. Three hots and a cot for a while. Though I don't think he's going to be charged, like Brandon will be, with kidnapping. I think he'll get charged with attempted murder for tampering with your car—and maybe reckless endangerment and mayhem. Not sure mayhem is a crime."

"But Brandon planned to blow up Pier 69."

"Yes. He did. The FBI is trying to find evidence that he had connections with Islamic militants in Malaysia. If that bomb had gone off, it would have been worse than the Boston Marathon, because he had weapons grade plastic explosives."

They walked around the side of the building to the backstage door. Davis stopped and pulled Grayce into his arms. "Honey, I'm sorry I brought up the conversation. Let's forget it for tonight."

"I agree. No more discussion. I'm enjoying being away from Seattle. Makes the unreal, grim experience seem further in the past than two weeks ago."

Grayce turned and spoke to the guard at the door. They were escorted into a bare, dimly lit, backstage area—a striking disparity from the audience's experience in the Center with lush, red velvet curtains, elegant chandeliers, and a sweeping staircase.

"Tell me again how James knows this dancer."

"James is friends with a lot of the boys at Pacific Northwest Ballet. Andrew was in the corps in Seattle, but left when he was offered a solo position with ABT. It's a big career step for him. He's an amazing dancer and an incredible actor. His talent is going to be used very well by ABT, which values both technical skill and emotional connection."

"Do I need to be jealous? And why do you call him a boy? How old is he?"

"No, you don't need to be jealous of Andrew. I'm not his style. And ballet company members are called boys and girls. It's tradition."

Andrew, a young lithe man, was dressed in sweats with a hoodie and down booties. He came from a stairwell behind them. He had taken class to warm up before the performance. He moved with energetic grace.

"Grayce, darling, it's wonderful to see you." He held her hands. "I'm sorry James isn't with you. I'd love for him to see me perform at the Kennedy Center. Not bad for a boy from Everett."

"Davis and I are thrilled to be in the audience. And thank you for taking time to show us backstage."

Andrew inspected Davis from his black Italian loafers to his

Armani tie. "James didn't exaggerate." He held his hand out. "Nice to meet you, Davis."

"Grayce, I can't believe it. James told me how you stopped a bomb threat and found a missing war veteran who was on the streets. He said you've become *Law and Order* of Seattle."

Grayce felt both her face warming and an urge to yell at James for spreading stories and exaggerating her talents. "I'm sure whatever James has told you, you should take with a giant—enormous—grain of salt."

She glanced at Davis with wide eyes, in a look of *Can you believe James?*

"James suggested I talk with you about a problem at PNB. A principal dancer believes someone is poisoning another dancer's pets to get promoted in the company. James said you'd be happy to help."

Grayce and Davis both let out a groan. "James!"

ACKNOWLEDGMENTS

Thank you to my extraordinary team of experts. Helen Fitzpatrick, Executive Director of Administration, Seattle Fire Department, who never stops sharing her incredible expertise. Karuna, my plot partner, who never stops with the brilliant ideas. Mike Hacker and Valerie Susan Hayward, my amazing editors, who never ask what the #*!* were you thinking? And to my support team who keep me writing. Maria Connor, Jen Rice, Cynthia Garlough, and my wondrous children.

A NOTE TO MY READERS

Dear reader,

Thank you for reading *Women Under Fire!* I hope you enjoyed it. If you did, please help others find it by writing a review!

Reviews mean so much to an independent author and I love reading them!

And if you sign up for my newsletter to see the latest news, and join my readers group to be the first to hear about special events, excerpts, and unseen previews!

Visit my website: http://www.jackidelecki.com to read more about the adventures of Grayce Walters, animal acupuncturist in *An Inner Fire*.

MEN UNDER FIRE: BOOK THREE

H ollie, Grayce's office assistant, stood on a stool and reached into the cupboard above the file cabinet. With her back to the door, Hollie was unaware of an audience.

Grayce was afraid to speak and startle Hollie in front of the new client—a wounded military dog and her handler.

Sergeant Welby's entire body tightened at the sight of Hollie in her short skirt. Grayce heard him take a deep breath.

Hollie hummed a Nirvana song as she searched in the back of the cupboard. Her tight skirt rode higher giving a full view of her upper thighs in fishnet stockings.

Under his breath, Sergeant Welby said something in a desperate tone. Grayce was pretty sure she heard. "Oh, hell."

Hollie turned quickly with the sound and almost fell backward into the cabinet.

"I didn't hear you come out of the office." Hollie jumped off the stool in one agile move unfazed by her high-heeled boots.

Hollie and the sergeant locked eyes for several seconds, neither uttering a sound. Grayce watched, fascinated. She could almost see the sparks flowing between them.

"Galachel!" The sergeant broke the awkward silence. His eyes were focused on Hollie's black t-shirt with a mythical female figure with flowing golden hair. Unlike last week's avenging goddess, this woman on Hollie's t-shirt was ephemeral and mystical.

Her chatty office assistant was dumbstruck. A wash of color crossed her cheeks. "You know...Galachel?" Her voice came out in a breathless whisper.

The sergeant angled his body closer to Hollie. "The radiant daughter."

The charge between the two people was electrifying. Grayce hated to interrupt the painfully wonderful moment.

"Hollie, can you give Talley and Sergeant Welby..."

"Please call me Nick." His lowered voice was focused toward Hollie.

Hollie looked young and sweet despite her heavy metal piercings and tattoos. Grayce sometimes forgot Hollie's young age.

"Can you make an appointment for Nick and Talley next week?" Grayce asked.

"Can do." Hollie bent over Talley, the devoted dog who had served with the sergeant, and rubbed her head. "What an amazing dog."

Talley, relaxed from the acupuncture treatment and sensing Hollie's empathy, raised her head to continue the petting.

Nick eased his tight control on Talley's lead. His face had softened, and his lips parted in a smile.

Hollie looked up into Nick's face and whatever she saw caused a blush to creep up her neck and face.

Grayce cleared her throat. "I'll look forward to seeing you next week, Nick and Talley."

As she walked back into her office, Grayce hummed "Smells Like Teen Spirit." Moments like this were important to savor. The universe had just provided a serendipitous path to help heal the wounded sergeant.

ABOUT THE AUTHOR

Jacki Delecki is a USA Today bestselling romantic suspense author whose stories are filled with heart-pounding adventure, danger, intrigue, and romance.

Her books have consistently received rave reviews for her three bestselling suspense series: Contemporary romantic suspense *The Impossible Mission Series*, featuring Special Force Operatives; *The Grayce Walters Series*, contemporary romantic suspense following a Seattle animal acupuncturist with a nose for crime; and *The Code Breakers Series*, Regency suspense set against the backdrop of the Napoleonic Wars.

Jacki's stories reflect her lifelong love affair with the arts and history. When not writing, she volunteers for Seattle's Ballet and Opera Companies, and leads children's tours of Pike Street Market.

To learn more about Jacki and her books and to be the first to hear about giveaways, join her newsletter found on her website.

f

IF YOU LOVED WOMEN UNDER FIRE YOU WILL ALSO ENJOY...

Grayce Walters Mystery series

An Inner Fire

Women Under Fire

Men Under Fire

Marriage Under Fire

A Marine's Christmas Wedding

The Grayce Walters Romantic Suspense Series 1-4

The Impossible Mission Romantic series

Mission: Impossible to Resist

Mission: Impossible to Surrender

Mission: Impossible to Love

Mission: Impossible to Forget

Mission Impossible to Wed

Mission: Impossible to Protect

Mission Impossible to Deny

The Impossible Mission Series Books 1-3

Code breaker Regency series

A Code of Love

A Christmas Code

A Code of the Heart

A Cantata of Love

A Wedding Code

A Code of Honor

A Holiday Code for Love

A Code of Wonder

A May Day Code for Love

A Code of Joy

A Secret Code

The Code Breakers Series Box Set

The Code Breakers Series: Holiday Romances

ISBN

POD 978-0-9899391-6-4

Ebook 978-0-9899391-7-1

Doe Bay Publishing, Seattle, Washington.

Cover Design and Interior format by Kim Killion.

Made in United States
Orlando, FL
20 April 2024

45987394R00147